PEARL OF MAGIC

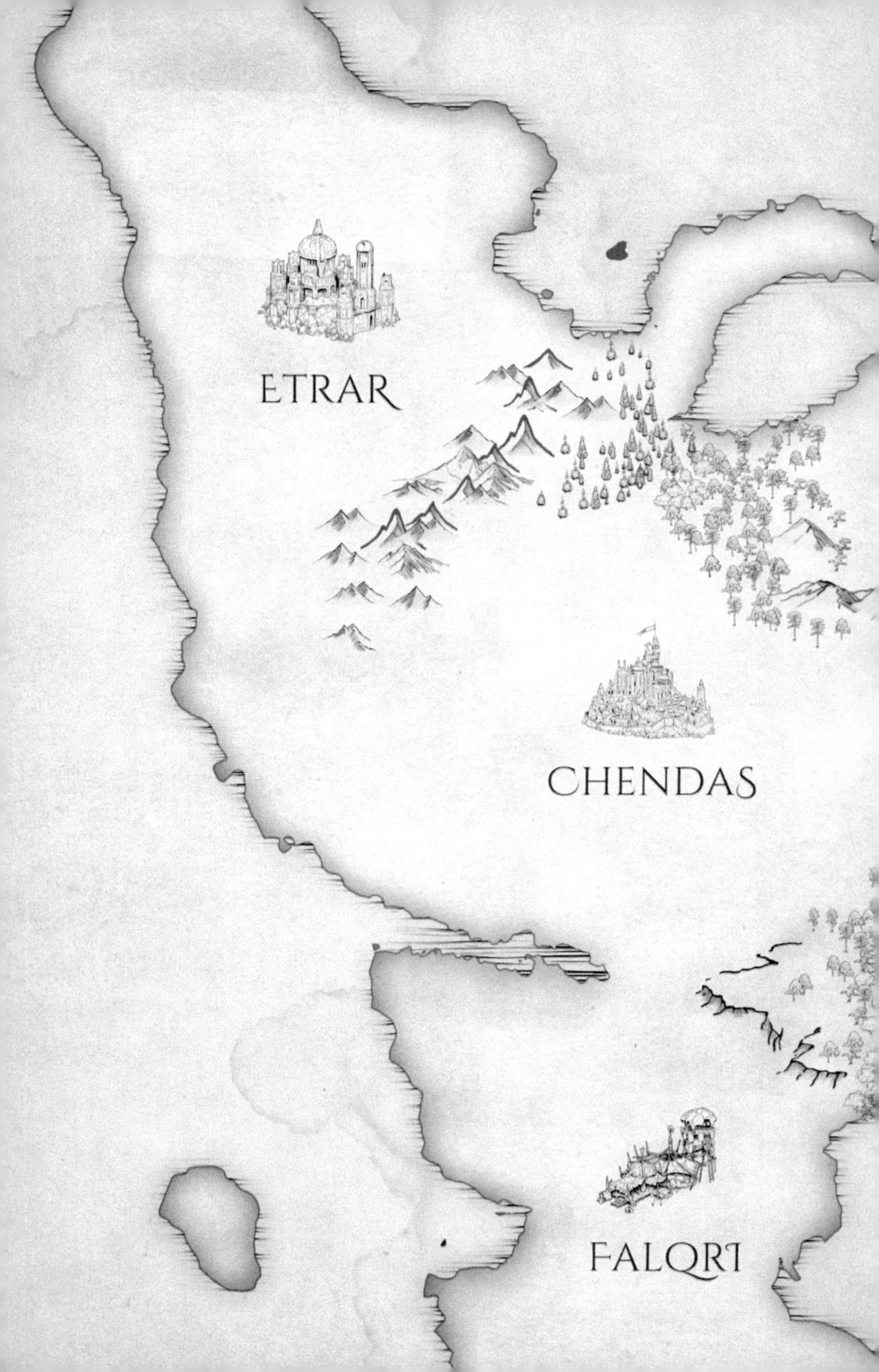

ETRAR
CHENDAS
FALQRI

ALLYS
ISELDIS
Isle of Exile

PEARL OF MAGIC
A LITTLE MERMAID ROMANCE

EMILY DEADY

Editor: M.S. Wordsmith

Cover Design: Covers by Combs

ISBN: 978-1-7349865-3-2

❀ Created with Vellum

For Ethan,
who always challenges me to see the bigger picture.

CHAPTER 1

"Erich, they are meeting without you!" Meena's sandals slapped against the stone floor of the castle hall as she chased her older brother.

Erich turned and waited for her to catch up. "Are you sure? Ian said he would invite me to the planning meeting." Erich excelled at bringing people together and making sure they all enjoyed themselves. Their older brother Ian would be an idiot to overlook his core strengths.

"Did he say 'a' planning meeting or 'the' planning meeting?" Meena skidded to a stop right before running into him.

Narrowing his eyes, Erich thought back to Ian's promise. His brother would never tell a lie, but he was not above twisting a few words to get his own way. "The sneak," Erich muttered. "He never intended for me to help at all, did he?"

"Steward Daniel and Miss Roth went upstairs ages ago." Meena gave him a gentle shove in the back, encouraging him to return down the hallway.

"Curses." Erich leaned his weight against her to remain in

place, biting his lower lip. If his older brother did not want him present, maybe he shouldn't push the matter. "Should I really go interrupt them?"

"Yes!" Meena dug her shoulder into his back, pushing against him with all her might. "You know Ian will royally mess this up—or it will royally mess *him* up. He needs you because you're so good at this."

"I am, aren't I?" Erich could not stop the smug grin spreading across his face. He took a quick step away from his sister, laughing as she stumbled forward from the lack of contact.

"Rude!" She slapped his shoulder. "I'll get you back for that later. Now, get up there and make sure this stuffy dance is going to be worth attending. If it's not fun, I'll personally hold you accountable!"

"Fine. Fine. I'll take this responsibility seriously." Erich threw up his hands in mock defeat, but the smile was still on his face.

Meena seemed unconvinced. "Like that's ever happened."

"You coming too?" Erich asked, ignoring her jab.

Meena's only response was the slapping of her sandals as she dashed away. Erich fell into a quick jog and followed her to the upper wing of the castle.

Outside his brother's study, Erich stopped to catch his breath. He had to approach this confidently or he would not be taken seriously. Looking down, he rearranged his purple vest. Confidence was all about clothing; looking impeccable would give him the extra boost needed to open that door and interrupt his brother's meeting.

Still nervous, he raised an eyebrow at Meena. Just because he offered his help didn't mean it would be accepted.

She nodded. "He needs us."

Erich took a deep breath and reached for the door. Meena grabbed his wrist before he could pull on its handle.

"Whatever you do," she hissed, "don't mention *her*."

Erich gave a single nod. "I may choose to be obnoxious, but I'm not that dumb," he whispered back.

Erich slammed open the study door with all the confidence of a twenty-year-old prince. "Sorry to keep you waiting." He flashed his most dashing smile. He knew it was dashing because he had spent quite some time perfecting it.

Three pairs of surprised eyes looked up at him.

Crown Prince Ian, his oldest brother, quickly schooled his surprise to indifference. "I don't remember inviting you," he said. "At least to this particular meeting."

"Do I mean so little to you?" Erich placed a hand over his heart as he sauntered inside and sprawled on the nearest empty chair.

Ian turned away, his lips pinched.

If they had been in private, Ian would have surely rolled his eyes. Never missing an opportunity to annoy his older brother, Erich decided to count that as a victory.

The other members of the room offered Erich a far more conciliatory welcome. Steward Daniel, who managed the daily operations of the castle, nodded curtly in his typical efficient fashion.

Miss Roth, the steward's second-in-command, smiled warmly. Erich grinned back at her. She'd always had a soft spot for him. At least she was on his side.

"So, what did I miss?" Erich asked as Meena settled in next to him.

The steward glanced toward Ian. He must have sensed the crown prince's discomfort.

Ian kept his arms crossed, avoiding eye contact with the steward and everyone else in the room.

Steward Daniel cleared his throat and turned his attention back to Erich. "We were just discussing whether the evening should start with supper or dancing."

"Dancing, of course," Erich quickly offered.

"But that will extend the length of the night," Ian replied, his eyes still plastered to the far wall.

"Exactly," Erich responded. "A few hours of dancing before supper will put everyone in a good mood and make sure they are hungry for all the delicious food."

"An excellent observation." Miss Roth nodded at Erich as she watched Ian carefully.

"This is *my* ball," Ian said, glaring at Erich. "And perhaps I prefer it to be as short as possible."

Erich shared a quick glance with Meena. This was exactly what they had hoped to avoid. It *was* Ian's ball, but it had been forced upon him.

"I am sorry, Ian," Erich said, empathizing with the difficult position his brother was in, "but this ball is supposed to be a night of celebration, bringing the people of Iseldis together during a difficult time. Opening the ball with a dance and saving the meal for later in the evening would make the whole event more festive and unitive." If everything in his life were festive and unitive, Erich would be a very happy man.

At his side, Meena nodded supportively.

Ian sighed deeply, as though his patience were being tried more than he could bear. Perhaps it was. "Thank you for stating facts I am well aware of."

Erich winced at the anything-but-thankful tone, but he kept a smile on his face. "I know you don't want to do this," he continued. "I would be happy to take care of the boring details for you."

Erich loved parties. He loved dancing, he loved music, and he loved the energy of a sparkling ballroom filled with excited people. Ian, however, preferred to lead councilors and advisors in long, complicated meetings—he was going to make a great king someday.

But their small kingdom was on the brink of war, a race of magic-wielders due to return to the continent in a year's time to enact revenge for their thousand-season exile.

In order to unite the kingdom and prepare for the looming invasion, Crown Prince Ian had been asked to host a ball and choose a wife. In the possible event of King Fred-erich and Queen Cara not surviving the attack, Ian's marriage would be essential to the stability of the kingdom.

As Meena had just reminded Erich, Ian's heart had been broken many seasons ago. Yet, the crown prince had agreed to this ball and future marriage out of his overzealous responsibility to his people and kingdom.

Erich truly felt sorry for his older brother and wanted to help him. If his help also ensured that the night of dancing would be as incredible as possible, that was just an extra thing to be thankful for.

"This is my ball." Ian's voice was diplomatic but firm. "I get to decide how it takes place."

"Brother, just because it is your ball does not mean it is your responsibility to plan every aspect of it," Erich pleaded. "All you really have to do is show up and—"

Meena jabbed Erich in the side. She could practically read his mind, which was quite fortunate. His next words would have been "and choose your future queen," and that would have made Ian more upset.

Personally, Erich did not think it quite so horrible a proposition. He would gladly marry any woman who loved dancing. What better place to find a girl who loved dancing than at a dance?

"I don't intend to plan everything," Ian responded. "But I do plan on ensuring that you two pests aren't given any chance to ruin it."

Erich inhaled, wishing he could respond in kind to his older brother's harsh words. But Ian was hurting, and Erich knew his words weren't intentional. That didn't mean he wasn't bothered by them, however.

"Ian, this is clearly making you miserable," Meena said, joining in the pleading. "Let us help you!"

"We know you are still missing Robin—" Erich started his plea with as much passion and empathy as he could muster, but Ian raised his voice before Meena could even jab his side again.

"This is my responsibility, and responsibility is not something I trust you with, Erich." Ian's usually calm voice had taken on a desperate edge.

Then Meena poked Erich in the side. Hard. He had mentioned the one name he was never, ever supposed to speak again.

"Well, then." Erich swallowed, his side and his pride both smarting. As much as he wanted to help Ian, he'd had enough rejection for one day. "I will leave you to it."

CHAPTER 2

"Goodnight, Celesta." Aizel hugged her sister, tucking the threadbare blanket closer around the younger girl and then kissing her on the forehead.

Celesta threw her arms around Aizel's neck.

Aizel squeezed her back, relishing every second of the warm contact.

Finally, when Celesta loosened her arms, Aizel sat up. Using their wordless language, Aizel opened her palm flat and touched her own cheek to imitate a person sleeping. Then, wiggling her fingertips, she made a wide arc above her head to signify the sparkling stars above. Finally, she kissed the back of her own thumb and pressed the kiss to Celesta's nose.

For Aizel, the motions were as habitual as speaking. To her, they meant: *Sleep well. The sparkling stars will watch over you. I love you.*

Celesta smiled in understanding, repeating the same gestures back to her.

Reaching up, Celesta held two fingers against Aizel's throat. *"Sing for me?"*

That was a request Aizel could not deny. Rearranging herself more comfortably on the edge of her sister's low, narrow bed, she inhaled deeply and closed her eyes.

Celesta cuddled up against her, close enough to feel the resonance in her chest and throat.

The low rumble of the sea's crashing waves drifted through the light paneled walls of their low island home. The steady rhythm of a tasker's gait sounded from the street on the other side of the house. One of these sounds brought comfort and peace; the other made her alert and uneasy.

Aizel focused on the sound of the sea, imagining its ebb and flow overpowering the tasker's footsteps.

Then, she began a slow melody her mother had taught her in the ancient words. Her grandmother had known their original meaning, but Aizel could not remember her Amma's translation. She still liked the sound of the ancient song, and it never failed to soothe her.

It was Celesta's favorite as well. Even though she could not hear the words, she was always calm and peaceful after Aizel sang it.

By the time she had finished the first verse, the tasker's footsteps had disappeared into the night and the only remaining sound was that of the sea.

Aizel exhaled, relishing the relaxation that spread from her scalp to her toes. If she could stop time, she would choose to live in this moment. Her body and mind were at peace, and her little sister was safe.

But the sun would rise tomorrow and she would be up before it, her body tense and alive and ready for work. And

Celesta's twelfth goldenreign was only a few months away. That would change everything.

"Shush!" a harsh whisper sounded through the woven reed door. "Are you daft? They are practically outside the door. Quiet your voice."

"Sorry, Mama," Aizel whispered, her relaxed muscles instantly tensing. She tightened her throat, as if blocking the words inside her would remind her not to speak—or sing. A Majis who used magic outside of their task would be forced to wear the necklace, and there was nothing Aizel hated more.

But if this was her last night with Celesta, she was happy to have risked it. Aizel leaned back down for one last hug. She had tears in her eyes that she needed to hide.

Her sister was more perceptive than most—since she had to rely on reading lips and facial expressions—and she would notice the tears immediately.

"I love you forever and always," Aizel whispered, her lips hidden from view. "I hope you never doubt that."

Celesta pushed against Aizel's shoulders to lift her from the second hug. The younger girl's face was pensive, and she ran her thumb under Aizel's eye.

Aizel blinked sheepishly. "I should have known better than to try and hide it from you," she whispered, signing their motion for an apology.

Celesta raised her eyebrows and lifted her palms face up.

"I'm just tired." Aizel answered her sister's signed question by both speaking and tilting her head into her hand. "They made me do extra dives today."

Celesta narrowed her eyes, shaking her head in disapproval. *Did you upset them again?* she asked with her hands.

Aizel shook her head, keeping her eyes steady. "They raised the quota again, and I had to go back down for more." It was mostly true, at least. Her sister didn't need to know she'd also given away two of her pearls to Sol while they were still under the surface.

"You gave yours away? Again?" Celesta raised her eyebrows.

Aizel smiled in defeat. Celesta could always see right through her. "Just two." She raised her hand, holding up two fingers as she spoke.

Celesta shook her head. *"Why is it that you always help everyone else, but you never let anyone help you?"*

Aizel nodded. "It was worth it. Sol has more mouths to feed with his father being sent to the shipyard."

"You're sweet on him." Celesta made a kissing motion as she teased her older sister.

Aizel shook her head. Sol was hardworking and kind, but he was constantly serious and only ever worried about the work he had to do. Not that she had time to be sweet on anyone.

Since the goldenreign of her twelfth year, she had worked as a diver—or "fish" as the Quotidian taskers called them. No matter how tumultuous the weather or the waves, she spent every day combing the bottom of the sea for oysters. And when she came back up, she was too exhausted to even think about being sweet on a boy. That was a luxury she would never be given.

But there was a luxury she planned on taking, if not for herself then for her sister and her parents.

"Good night, my shining star." Aizel reached down and touched her sister's cheek, committing it to memory.

"Rest well." Celesta cradled Aizel's hand against her face.

With a final smile, Aizel stood and left the room before fresh tears could spill.

Tonight, she was leaving.

CHAPTER 3

Erich's heart pounded as he stood by his brother's bed. Ian's ball had been a wonderful success—despite his older brother's attempt to keep it as controlled as possible. Erich had lost himself in the energy of the music and the dancing, leading partner after partner through the swirling chaos on the polished dance floor. He could have gone on forever, smiling and laughing and dancing.

His only complaint was that the evening had been cut short. Not that he blamed Ian for that. A Majis had infiltrated the attendants and attacked their brother Aden.

Aden was the third son of the family, directly older than Erich by two years. At the moment, he was peacefully sleeping in his own bed. But he had been transformed into some sort of human-shaped beast, and they had no idea what would happen when he awoke. Two of the palace guards flanked his bed just in case he proved to act as wild as he appeared.

Erich felt completely helpless as he stared at him. No one

deserved this, least of all bookish Aden. He glanced around the room, eager to find something else—anything else—to occupy his mind.

Ian ran a hand through his hair. Erich thought he looked slightly green, as though he were about to be sick. "This is all my fault," Ian muttered to himself. "The attack was aimed at me."

Erich's jaw tensed.

He was no good in situations like this. His biggest strength was that he knew exactly what his own strengths were—a fact he was quite proud of.

He was very good at engaging with others and making sure everyone was excited and happy. He prided himself on turning the most uninspiring and stressful situations into enjoyable experiences. That particular strength was no use at the moment. No one was supposed to be enjoying themselves when their brother could be dying. This was a tragic situation, one that called for feeling sad and morose.

He had nothing to offer here.

Feeling overwhelmed by uselessness, Erich quietly worked his way around the edge of the room toward the half-open door.

Before he could make his escape, a whispered conversation reached his ears from just outside in the hallway.

"Councilor Munney is safely secured, Your Majesty," a voice reported.

"He does not deserve the title of Councilor," Erich's father replied. "The only title he deserves are words I cannot utter in front of my wife."

"Frederich." Erich could hear the quiet reprimand in his mother's voice.

"He's a monster, Cara," King Frederich said. "Only a

monster could willingly create another monster. I knew the Majis were capable of horrors, but this . . . it is less than human."

"Do *not* call our son a monster." His mother's voice caught in a strangled sob.

Erich had rarely heard his mother cry, and the sound made him want to both hug her and run as far away from her as possible. If Queen Cara was crying, the situation was truly dire.

Erich's father felt the same way. "If Munney were not under Gareth's jurisdiction, I would go to the dungeons now and strangle him for this." Erich had never heard his level-headed father sound this raw with anger.

Erich couldn't walk out the door while such an intimate conversation was taking place just outside of it. He bit his lower lip as panic swelled inside him. He had to get out of this suffocating room.

"Frederich." His mother's voice held a note of warning. "Justice and mercy make you a worthy king. Not anger."

"Mercy? This monster deserves no mercy. Some lives are more important than others, and his is worthless. I hope Gareth can see that justice is properly done. I will be asking for retribution."

"I am not disagreeing with you. But Aden must be our focus now," Queen Cara said.

Moving away from the door and back into the center of Aden's bedroom, Erich considered his father's words. King Frederich had always taught his sons that the mark of a good ruler was balancing the tension between justice and mercy. He had never heard his father eschew mercy completely for the sake of justice. But his father had also never encountered a Majis before . . .

Looking at his cursed brother, Erich felt the same anger toward the evil Munney, the same desire to see him punished.

Aden stirred on the bed, his breath coming out in a deep, powerful rumble. Ian and Erich tensed.

"Should I call more guards to help restrain him?" Erich asked as they waited to see if Aden would move again.

Ian looked up from his place by the bed. "No." Brow furrowed, he glanced across the room. "There are four of us here now, and father is outside the door. Besides, he's going to wake up fine." Ian sounded as though he was trying to convince himself. "He has to," he muttered under his breath, "or I'll never forgive myself."

Erich's heart ached when he heard the pain in Ian's voice. "Of course he will wake up fine," Erich reassured. "He may *look* worse than before, but perhaps he'll wake up with a better attitude." Erich attempted to smile with his words, hoping that a little bit of humor would ease the tension in Ian's face.

"Are you really trying to jest right now?" Ian's voice hitched as it filled the room.

"Now is not the time, son." Directly behind Erich, King Frederich's voice sounded deep and low.

Erich quickly turned around, unaware his parents had entered the room.

"I wasn't . . ." Erich started to defend himself, but the disappointment and reproach in his father's eyes cut him short. "I was just trying to help." He sighed and dropped his eyes to the floor. The panicked feeling of helplessness grew thick in his throat. "I . . . my throat hurts. I need to find some water." Speeding away from his potentially dying brother's bed, Erich fled from the stifling weight of his family's disapproval.

Across the hall, in the safety of his room, Erich threw himself on his own bed without bothering to remove the decorated clothing he'd worn to the dance.

His mind refused to sleep, but there was nothing left to be done—other than lying on his bed feeling miserable and useless.

His father had already sent messengers to the Council in Chendas. They knew the most about the Majis and their magic. Hopefully, they would know enough to reverse the curse. Physicians had also been summoned from every corner of the kingdom. The only thing they could do now was wait.

Erich flung his pillows across the room, one by one, until his bed was empty.

After tossing and turning in discomfort, he got up and gathered the pillows back to his bed—only to repeat the process.

He didn't know how long he'd been waiting in silent misery when he heard frantic hoofbeats pounding in the private courtyard below his window.

He sat up immediately.

The sky outside was still completely dark. Whoever was arriving in such a hurry had something important to share.

Erich quickly left his room, glad to have found a purpose for the boundless energy that wouldn't stop coursing through him.

He skidded to a halt in front of his father's study. Normally, his father didn't mind his sons participating in meetings. But everything about this night was unusual, and

Erich could still feel the guilt his father's reproachful eyes had instilled in him.

"There's been an attack on the coastline near the old monastery." The messenger must have just begun his report. Erich could hear him fairly well through the wooden door.

It was the second time that night he was listening in on conversations uninvited, but he had no problem pushing away the guilt for doing so.

"The attack is definitely from the magic-wielders," the messenger continued. "They are hurling some sort of fire spheres from their ship to the monastery and the coast. I left as soon as the attack began. But two other unrecognized ships were sighted farther out at sea and are working their way closer to shore."

"How many soldiers are stationed at the monastery and village?" King Frederich asked.

"Barely more than thirty," the voice of General Zimri answered. The older man had overseen the Iseldis armies since before Erich was born. "They could likely call on an additional forty or fifty farmers and fishermen in the area, but they would not be able to arm them."

"Especially against a magic attack," King Frederich said. "That would be a slaughter. No, we need to send reinforcements now."

"I will prepare to leave immediately."

"Thank you for your willingness, old friend, but let us discuss this for a moment further to decide whether it is prudent for you to go yourself." Erich could hear the desperate rhythm of his father's fingers drumming across his desk. "With the attack here at the palace mere hours ago, this was obviously a coordinated effort. I don't know where they will strike next. Your knowledge and skill might be best served here, to lead the larger strategic defense."

"Let me call for one of the captains of the elite guard, then," Zimri responded. "As next in the line of command, this task would fall to them."

Erich reached for the door handle. Finally, something he could do. Despite his young age, he was one of the highest-ranking captains.

"That would be Ian?" King Frederich asked.

Erich pulled his hand back. Ian was one of the few who outranked him.

"Who else is available?" King Frederich continued. "Ian is . . . perhaps not the proper choice at this time."

Erich couldn't agree more. His oldest brother had been through quite a bit that night. With his sense of responsibility toward Aden's condition, he likely wouldn't be able to focus on the task ahead if separated from him.

"We could send Erich."

Erich grasped the door handle, a "yes" on his lips.

"Is there anyone else?" His father's voice froze him in place.

"The other two captains were sent with the messengers to Chendas," Zimri said.

His father sighed.

Erich took a step back, wanting to disappear before anyone discovered he was there.

"Erich has performed admirably under my command, my lord." General Zimri spoke respectfully but confidently.

The kind words from the man who was like a grandfather to him rooted Erich to the spot. He could listen for just a moment longer.

"He has rightfully earned his rank as captain through his own merit," Zimri continued.

"I admit it's hard for me to imagine my youngest son carrying this much responsibility, but I do realize my perception is limited."

Erich felt pained by his father's words, despite his culpability in the matter. As the fourth son, Erich had practically encouraged his father to consider him impulsive and somewhat immature. It had helped him stand out and feel like his own person, especially when Ian, Onric, and Aden were all incredibly skilled and mature in their ways. It had been easier to play up his role as the spoiled youngest than try to compete with his older brothers.

"He is your son and namesake, Frederich. Your concern is understandable. I cannot guarantee his safety, but I do wholeheartedly vouch for his competence." Zimri's words once again filled Erich with comfort and pride.

He could do this. He wanted to do it. He wanted to make his father proud.

He pushed open the door and walked into the room, pretending he had not been standing outside since the beginning of the conversation. "I heard a messenger arrived in the courtyard. Is something wrong?"

A look of guilt flashed across his father's face, as though he wondered whether Erich had heard his earlier words. Erich pretended not to notice, but he was glad to have seen it.

"The Majis have launched an attack on the coastline," King Frederich informed him.

Erich feigned shock. "No!"

"General Zimri plans to immediately send you to the old monastery with reinforcements. Are you up to the task?" His father's words placed the responsibility entirely on Zimri's shoulders.

Erich stood up to his full height. "Yes, I am. I can do this." He attempted to fold his arms, but the sprout-green tassels hanging off his sleeves tangled with each other and stopped the motion. Wishing he had changed from his dancing clothes, he smoothly grabbed his left wrist in his right hand instead and stood at attention, exuding as much confidence as he could.

King Frederich exhaled and buried his face in his hands. "I cannot lose another son this night."

His father's simple words soothed Erich's hurt feelings.

"Then send me, Your Majesty," Zimri said.

"No," Erich cut in. "I understand you wish to keep me out of danger, but nowhere is safe anymore. We were just attacked here, in this very castle. I am twenty years old, fully trained, and have the additional benefit of being a direct representative of the royal family. This is my responsibility."

King Frederich lifted his head and gazed intently at Erich. "So be it." He stood up from his desk to address the general. "Gather a full contingent if you can spare it. They leave at once."

The general nodded and left the room, his booted feet thumping against the hard floor.

Erich moved to follow him, but his father placed a hand on his shoulder.

"Be safe." King Frederich's voice was low.

Erich nodded. "I will."

"And Erich?" his father's voice called after him before he could slip out the door. "Wear your uniform."

Erich rolled his eyes at the dark hallway. "Yes, Father, I will." He was not a child anymore.

Mere minutes later, Erich was on his horse, riding through the courtyard gates into the night. He was wearing the gray uniform of the Iseldis guard, but the stiff vest was hidden underneath his own thick fur cape. The night air was cold, and it would only become more so as they neared the sea.

If they pushed themselves as hard as possible, they would reach the shore before dawn.

Erich leaned over his horse, ducking his head against the western winds. While he had spent the night dancing and then worrying over Aden, he wasn't even close to exhaustion.

He was so ready for this.

The muscles in his body were relaxed but poised. The horse carried his weight, but his legs and chest responded elegantly to the swaying motion of the galloping animal. He felt alive, ready for an exciting adventure.

Erich had trained his whole life for this moment, knowing that he would be defending his kingdom from the cruel and powerful magic-wielders that haunted even the most ancient of legends. He was a captain of the elite guard. Though he was only twenty, he had spent the last six summers rigorously training in the Falqri desert. There was a reason his body could endure a night of dancing before effortlessly mounting a warhorse and making all haste to the sea to reinforce their defenses.

Erich was ready.

CHAPTER 4

*A*izel's neck twisted uncomfortably against her lumpy pillow. It was her own fault. She was the one who had torn open a corner of the stitching to remove the scraps of fabric and old feathers that made up the pillow itself. She had replaced the stuffing with a few essential items for her escape.

When she was sure her parents were deeply asleep, Aizel slipped out of bed. Grabbing the makeshift pillow sack, she stepped silently across the sandy floor and slipped through the woven door of their small home.

When she was a child, the Quotidian taskers had enforced a strict curfew every evening. Now, they kept everyone working during all hours of the night and day, which made her current mission far easier. It was hard to shake old habits, though, and merely stepping outside after dark put her on edge.

No one seemed to notice her darting from shadow to shadow as she made her way down the dilapidated alley.

The village was surrounded by a tall sandstone wall, which was said to keep the waves out—although Aizel had always felt it was more intended to keep the Majis in.

Slipping into a line of tired workers, she kept her head down and shuffled through the guarded western gate. Once outside the village wall, she peeled away from the group. Her bare feet were silent on the sand. No one wore shoes on Istroya because they hampered movement on the soft, shifting ground.

Things were going too easily, but her senses remained on high alert. The taskers were not incredibly concerned about someone escaping from the island as it was impossible to do so without a ship. And it was impossible to get a ship close to Istroya due to the shallow reefs surrounding the island. The main port up north was more heavily guarded.

She had made contact with a member of the River's Talon several seasons prior and arranged for them to smuggle Celesta off the island. Sadly, they had never arrived. Aizel could only assume something had happened to her contact, Peter, since she hadn't been able to get through to him again. She hoped that was not the case, but she could think of no other explanation.

So, Aizel planned her own escape. She would find the leader of the River's Talon—someone named Robin—and come back for Celesta and their parents. With the upcoming Quotidian attacks, she was running out of time.

A single guard patrolled the long, accessible length of the shore. Waiting for him to turn his back to her, she lingered in the shadow of the village wall.

She reached into her sack and pulled out a small vial. It was carved from the interior of a mollusk shell, which were easy to find on the shoreline, and it had the familiar iridescent shimmer of a pearl. She unlatched its intricate metal clasp, then removed the cap from the vial and dabbed a tiny amount of fragrant oil onto her fingertips.

Rubbing the oil around the base of her nose, she began to hum the tune her mother and grandmother had taught her. The crashing waves only a short distance away drowned out the noise of her song.

Despite its familiar floral scent, the powerful aroma added to the lightheadedness she already felt.

As a diver, she used the oil daily in order to breathe underwater. Extracted from the seeds of the Istroya fruit, the oil was scented with the essence of the lotus flower. Because it enhanced a magic user's ability, it was a highly regulated substance. Outside of their dives, the Majis were not allowed to own it, have it, or use it.

Aizel had spent weeks secretly saving minuscule drops from her daily ration to save up the small amount of oil in her mother's heirloom pearlescent vial. Since she hadn't told her parents of her plan, she felt a little guilty about taking her mother's small bottle. They would have certainly tried to stop her, or they would have insisted on coming as well—which would have been worse. Aizel was willing to risk her own life, but she would not be responsible for putting someone she loved in danger.

The guard was drawing nearer. She froze, silencing her song.

Objects themselves were not magical. But, depending on the amount of harmony within an object, it could channel magic better or worse. Lotus flowers were highly regarded among the Majis because they grew in the muddiest waters to emerge with beauty and color. Beauty balanced the mundane.

The taskers allowed parents to teach their children how to use magic, but it was strictly forbidden to pass on the traditions behind it. That hadn't stopped Aizel's mother from whispering stories to her in the dark of night, huddled under blankets, just as her mother had done with her.

The guard reached the end of the beach and turned back around. When his back was turned, Aizel quietly let out the breath she had not realized she'd been holding.

She slipped the vial back into her sack, which she then secured tightly around her waist. Fortunately, it was small as she had very few belongings to bring with her.

Before she could overthink her final move, Aizel sprinted silently to the open water. As she ran across the beach, she swooped down and picked up a few handfuls of seaweed that had washed ashore.

Her heart was pounding so quickly she felt it would escape from her chest.

She knew she must be mad for even attempting this. Her father said it took over a week for a ship to sail from the mainland. She was about to undertake that same journey—swimming—in the span of a night.

If she failed? She would be stranded in the middle of the sea.

Slipping off her outer layer of clothing, she tossed it onto the sand behind her. Hopefully, in the morning, when they discovered she was missing, they would assume she had drowned. If the taskers thought she had escaped, her family could be in danger.

Besides, it would be easier to swim in the single layer of her brown underdress.

The water swirling around her ankles was bitterly cold. She wanted to stand in it until her legs adjusted to the new temperature—or at least went numb—but she didn't have the time. The guard could turn around and scan the area any second. Dark though it was, she needed to be under the surface before that happened.

She plunged into the icy depths, her lungs seizing up with shock as her body adjusted to the cold. She hated the feeling of water washing over her dry scalp. It felt like it was sending shivers of ice into her mind.

For a moment, her body refused to respond to her command, and she wondered if she had actually frozen.

She tried to inhale through her nose, but nothing happened. Breaking waves rolled over her, tossing her body against the hard sand below.

Pushing away from the ground with her feet, she propelled herself headfirst into the waves to get to the open water. The physical motion restored some warmth to her insides as the freezing water finally numbed her skin.

Having adjusted to the shock, Aizel's lungs begged for air. Fighting her natural instinct to resurface and breathe, she inhaled through her nose.

Instead of drowning in saltwater, she inhaled air as the oil she had applied to her nostrils worked its magic. It felt slightly strained, as though she were breathing through a layer of heavy fabric, but at least she was breathing.

As her body adjusted to the shock of the temperature and the slower breathing pattern, she felt calmer. She had made it out of the house, past the guard, and into the open sea.

Only one more part of her plan remained to be carried out.

Swimming back up to the surface, she kept her head below the water line and tossed the strands of seaweed around her neck so they would not float away.

She had chosen tonight because the clear skies above boasted a full moon. Her legs dancing beneath her with the ease of a practiced skill, she carefully held her arms above the water. Reaching back into her soaked pack, she retrieved the small bottle once again.

Rather than open the vial, she held it up over her head, making sure not to block the glass handle. She twisted it until a single facet of the handle caught a ray of moonlight. The light streamed through the glass prism, breaking into a rainbow of colors.

Taking care not to break the reflection, she redirected the flow of light deep into the dark sea below her.

She was trying to attract a sunfish, a type of large fish she had discovered during her dives. They lived deep in the cold depths of the sea but eagerly swam to the surface every morning to warm themselves in the light of the sun.

The rays of the moon were not quite as strong, but hopefully they would do the trick.

After flashing the light into the water for a few moments, Aizel slipped the vial back into the sack around her waist. She grabbed the seaweed from around her neck and then sank back under the surface.

A few moments later, she saw a large shadow swimming toward her through the gloomy water. As the fish drew nearer, it split apart and two giant sunfish circled around her, their fist-sized eyeballs peering at her curiously.

Aizel floated in the water, waving her arms as gently as she could to keep herself in place without frightening the two massive fish.

She recognized Mola—the one she had befriended—by the indent in his upper fin. Both fish were shaped like large, round shields. They were as tall as she was and quite a bit longer. Viewed from the front, however, they were quite thin. Fins equal to the height of the fish itself protruded from the top and bottom, giving it a balanced silhouette.

Mola stopped circling her and nudged his massive face closer to her body.

He was clearly here for the seaweed treat he knew she had brought him.

She swung the slimy plant out away from her body and released it, leaving it suspended in the water between them.

With surprising swiftness, the two fish dove toward it. They quickly chomped it down.

When she didn't produce another strand of seaweed, the other fish lost interest and swam away, but Mola resumed swimming in circles around her. She reached out to scratch the thick scales above his eyes as she had often done before. He stopped swimming to give her a better angle for scratching.

When he was quite still, she propelled herself upward, slowly swinging a leg over the top of his body as though he were a horse. He remained still, not seeming to mind her presence.

When she had run into Mola two years prior, he had been a playful young fry and often sought her out from among the divers. She'd had no idea then, of course, that she would eventually attempt to swim across the sea with him, but she was incredibly thankful for the trust they had developed.

Leaning back so that her spine was pressed against his tall fin, she reached down and scratched the top of his head. Sitting still in the buoyant water, her body gently tried to rise back up to the surface, but she squeezed Mola lightly with her knees to keep herself in place. He sat still for a few moments longer, gently swaying in the water. Eventually, he must have realized the comfortable scratches he was receiving were not going anywhere. He started to swim forward.

Aizel kept up the comfortable rhythm. As the fish moved, the water naturally pushed her back against his tall, firm fin, and she was able to relax her knees, held in place simply by the constant pressure.

However, Aizel quickly realized Mola was traveling along the shoreline rather than away from it.

She lowered her left hand down his side and scratched harder, stopping all motion with her right hand.

As she'd hoped, Mola leaned into her scratches, which redirected him to head in the proper direction.

"Ha!" Aizel nearly choked herself with a triumphant underwater yell as Mola gathered momentum, and she settled herself in for a long underwater ride.

CHAPTER 5

*E*rich was not ready.

Standing on the deck of a rolling ship, he watched in horror as the water below him came alive. It tossed them up and then disappeared, leaving the massive warship to fall through the air as though it were lighter than a child's plaything.

Seasoned sailors screamed in fear, grabbing onto anything in sight to avoid falling overboard.

Erich had not even seen the enemy yet, but the effects of their capricious magic were already devastating.

Upon arriving at the monastery, he had boarded the final remaining vessel to fend off the vicious attack of raining fire-spheres that were coming from an unrecognized ship at sea.

That ship had quickly disappeared when they'd set out after it, and the water itself had turned on them instead. It was clearly being controlled—no normal sea storm played games like these.

"Turn back!" Erich yelled in an effort to make his voice audible above the crash of the waves, the screams of the sailors, and the groaning of the wood.

Clutching at a piece of fallen rigging, he attempted to cross the deck of the ship.

As he made his way, the water calmed. Seizing the unexpected moment, Erich dashed across the ship toward the captain, who had tied himself to the ship's wheel.

"Turn back!" Erich yelled again. "Our men's lives are not worth it. They have the advantage at sea. We will have to find a way to fight them from land."

The captain merely nodded in response as he threw the weight of his body against the wheel to turn the rudder.

Erich grabbed the railing to brace himself for the next attack.

The water remained calm.

Peering out into the rising sun, Erich tried to locate the ship they'd been chasing, but the horizon was clear.

His stomach tumbled. It felt as though the ship were still sinking, even though the horizon remained the same.

"Are we . . . still falling?" he asked, looking down at his feet. He immediately wished he could take his words back. Of course they weren't falling; he was just experiencing a twinge of seasickness.

"Look to starboard!" The captain's gruff voice carried above the high screeching of the frightened men.

Erich glanced back up, his eyes following the rising line of the horizon.

The line where the sea met the sky was moving . . . it covered the newly risen sun, blocking out the fragile light of the morning sky, and raced toward them as a wall of shadow.

Erich's neck had craned backward by the time he realized

what was happening. The enemy hadn't stopped their attack. They had merely drawn all the water they could into one area to create a single giant, colossal wave.

Dozens of commands ran through Erich's head, but nothing had prepared him for this. "Brace yourselves!" He wanted to shout something helpful, to make a plan, to get these men to safety. But there was nothing they could do against the wave rolling toward them, gaining height and momentum as it sped through the vast volume of available water.

The water pushing the wave from behind finally swelled over the top of the rolling monstrosity, surging upward in a thunderous crash of white foam as it broke.

In the next moment, the ship's deck was flying above Erich's head. It made a deafening boom that drowned out the sounds of the screaming sailors.

As he sank into the water, everything went silent.

CHAPTER 6

When she finally noticed the first rays of sunlight, Aizel felt as though she had lived through a thousand lifetimes.

Her body was not new to exhaustion—the taskers had seen to that—but guiding Mola through the waters while keeping their path straight by watching the hazy stars above the surface had taxed her completely.

She was cold, tired, and struggling to breathe the limited air the seal provided her.

Fortunately, the arrival of the sun prompted Mola to swim up to the surface in search of heat. For a short moment, Aizel's head was pushed above the water. Then she splashed back down as Mola flipped onto his side seeking maximum sun exposure.

Aizel quickly righted herself and scrambled to reach for him, pulling herself back out above the surface as they floated side by side.

"Thank you, Mola," she said, giving him another scratch.

"You swam fast and well. I could not have done this without you."

Soon, she would be free.

She would make sure Celesta was safe—forever—or she would die trying.

When she was a child, Aizel had not known that her life was difficult. Working from dawn to dusk and going hungry had been her normal.

It was not until Celesta—sweet, funny, innocent Celesta —had become Aizel's little sister and best friend that Aizel had begun to question the reality around her.

Because Celesta could not hear, she could not learn the proper songs to channel magic. And the taskers had no use for a Majis who could not control magic.

Most Majis remained silent at the risk of angering a tasker, so they had been able to keep Celesta's difference a secret. But she was nearly twelve, and soon the taskers would discover that Celesta was quotidian. They would probably send her directly to the water caves to mine for rare minerals. No one who went to the water caves lasted long. Or they would keep her alive for the Quotidian men at the northern port, which was a fate worse than death. And, from what she'd heard, no one lasted long there either.

No, Aizel would let neither fate befall her beloved sister and best friend. Even though she was somewhere in the middle of the sea beside a giant sea creature she could not communicate with, she was farther from Istroya than any Majis had ever been. Except for those who had escaped with the River's Talon, of course. She had to succeed.

She had no idea how far she had come, but without the stars to guide her way, she could no longer chart her course toward land.

Aizel flipped onto her back, keeping her shoulders positioned over Mola's sunbathing body. She noted the locations of the disappearing moon and rising sun.

There was no landmark anywhere on the horizon she could use to reference her direction. For now, she would have to do her best to continue moving away from the eastern morning sun.

Suddenly, her small hopes disappeared as the emptiness of her surroundings sent a moment of panic into her tired mind. She was going to die here, alone, in the middle of the ocean.

Even though her face was above the water, she struggled to breathe, feeling crushed, stifled, and out of control. She might be far, far away from Istroya, but she still sensed the oppressive feeling of Quotidian magic and the taskers' chaos that had drained the life from within her.

She felt as helpless as she had all those years ago when the taskers had affixed a white ribbon around her neck, silencing her voice to prevent her from using her magic against them.

She felt as though she were sinking.

Clutching onto Mola, she looked around her. The water was fine.

But Mola wasn't. Mola felt it, too.

The giant sunfish deftly flipped back into a vertical position. Water churned around him, separating them.

Aizel kicked her feet, trying to reposition herself. Instinctively, she breathed through her nose. Saltwater filled her lungs, stinging the back of her throat. The seal must have broken. It sometimes disappeared quickly when exposed to air.

She hastily broke above the surface again, coughing and choking.

Mola was frantic, his eyes rolling back and forth as he rotated his body on a vertical axis. He grabbed her tunic in his mouth and began to swim down, back to the safe depths.

Unable to breathe underwater, she frantically pushed herself away from him, trying to remove her clothing from his teeth. Her motions only frightened the poor fish more, and he held on tighter as he swam down, down, down. His safety was now dangerous for her—but of course, Mola didn't understand that.

The water swirled around them as though they were still at the surface. Aizel felt the pressure in her ears grow more intense than she had ever experienced.

Her lungs burned.

Bracing her feet on Mola, she shoved off against him. Thankfully, the threadbare fabric of her skirt gave way, and she quickly pushed herself toward the light.

The ascent felt so much longer than going down, but she attributed it to her desperate need to breathe.

Finally, her head surfaced, and she breathed in desperate gulps of precious air.

When she wiped the wet hair from her face, the first thing she saw was land. But she had no time to rejoice in her success.

The shoreline was so far below her that the buildings looked like small sandcastles.

She was riding the ridge of the tallest wave she had ever seen, and it was carrying her with surprising swiftness toward the shore.

From her vantage point, she could see two ships. One was behind her, and it had the familiar look of the ships that sailed to the port of Istroya. Only taskers rode those ships.

On the other side of the wave, close to the shore, she saw

another ship, its style and shape unfamiliar to her. She had no idea who was on the second ship. Not that it mattered. In a few moments, it would be crushed in the jaws of the wave she was riding.

As soon as she'd registered these thoughts, the tension of the water below her changed. Her view of the land and ships disappeared as white bubbling foam erupted around her. Some invisible force had compelled the water behind her to crest the wave, rolling it in on itself.

Having spent most of her life in the sea, Aizel was able to ride the wave rather than get sucked down into it.

Cutting through the thunderous noises, an earsplitting screech reached her as the unfamiliar ship crumpled beneath the crashing water's weight.

Without stopping to think, she plunged headfirst into the wave itself and rushed toward the sinking ship.

She had no time to sing the magic seal that allowed her to breathe underwater back into place, but she was still an expert diver.

Boards, ropes, and bodies swirled around her as she neared the destroyed ship. Many of the men were already stretching toward the surface, kicking their way back up. She glanced downward, looking for someone who needed her help.

A young man was sinking swiftly into the darkness below. He seemed to be stuck on a large piece of the broken mast that was dragging him down.

With a powerful kick, Aizel followed him into the darkness.

He was struggling to disentangle himself from the rigging attached to the mast. Ropes twisted around his right arm and tightened further as he tried to tug himself free.

She reached out for him, briefly catching his frantic gaze.

Staring up at her in disbelief, his large brown eyes were filled with a desperate plea.

He was perhaps her age, but the fear on his face made him seem even younger.

She grabbed his arm and attempted to pull him back up, but the heavy mast weighed him down.

She plucked at the web of ropes, pulling them off his arm one by one. Her lungs were already burning, and they had a long way up to get back to the surface—if she could free him in time. As her body cried for air, she wanted to take the ropes all at once and rip them away, but she knew that would only make matters worse.

At first, the young man helped her with his free hand, but after they had removed about five of the dozen loops, his hand stilled, floating eerily in the water.

No, no, no! Aizel thought. *Stay with me.*

Finally, once she had removed a few more strands, the rigging loosened enough to shake him free.

Come on, she urged inside her mind, willing him to stay alive. *Just a little longer.*

Grabbing the back of his shirt, she swam toward the surface once again.

He was heavy, but the water helped to buoy him up.

Her mind screamed for air, telling her to open her mouth and breathe, so she distracted herself by talking to the stranger with her thoughts. *This is not the end. Stay with me, friend. You are too young to die.*

For a moment, she wondered if he was also a Quotidian tasker, and the thought alone made her want to drop him. But perhaps that was simply because he was weighing her down and her mind was playing tricks on her to help her get to the surface and survive.

She had to survive.

She still had to save Celesta.

With that final thought spurring her on, she propelled herself toward the surface with another powerful kick.

At the last moment, her body betrayed her, and she inhaled through her nose just before her head reached the open air. As she curled into a coughing fit, her legs swam below her in their practiced pattern. Somehow, she managed to keep the stranger's head above water as well as her own. It was no easy feat as he wasn't carrying any of his own weight.

Positioning herself below him, she swam quickly to the shore. The water had carried them quite a distance from the main wreckage, and she instinctively continued to move away from it.

She needed to avoid the more populated areas if she wanted to stay free.

Dragging the man by his underarms, she pulled him ashore onto a secluded section of the beach. He was exceptionally tall and she was beyond exhausted, but she somehow managed to get him safely away from the lapping waterline. A quick glance told her the tide was receding, so he would be safe from the water's clutches for now.

The gentle swish of the shallow water mocked her with its calmness, as if it were an entirely separate entity than the vicious ocean. She ignored it, focusing on the drowning man in her arms.

Leaning over him, she pressed her hands against his chest with all her weight.

Water dribbled from his mouth. His hair was dark, like the taskers'. Her hands froze above his chest for the briefest moment as she realized she was saving the life of someone who would never do the same for her.

She blinked away the thought, leaning back onto his chest to help him expel the water from his lungs.

She dropped her eyes from his face so she wouldn't be tempted to abandon her task again. He was wearing a heavy gray shirt that fitted his tall, lean frame well. A fancily embroidered symbol rested over his heart. It looked official, like something a Quotidian soldier would wear.

With an interior groan, she looked back up at his face. His skin was turning gray, matching the shirt he wore.

Perhaps it was too late.

She felt vulnerable, sitting on the edge of the beach in open view. Search parties would surely be combing the area soon, looking for survivors.

Aizel needed to be far from here when that happened. The line of bushes further inland offered some coverage; or she could jump back into the sea and swim further up the shore.

But she could not leave the young stranger to his death without trying one more thing. Reaching into the sopping wet sack still bound to her side, she pulled out the vial of oil.

It likely wouldn't work, but she had to try.

Dabbing some oil onto her fingertips, she spread it over the base of his nose, quietly humming.

Then she pressed onto his chest again, forcing more water from his lungs.

With a sudden lurch, his body jolted to life and he coughed, gagging on the water in his mouth as he attempted to lift his head.

"Hello?" Aizel asked. "Can you hear me?"

The man continued to cough, but his eyes remained closed.

She exhaled in relief.

He was breathing on his own.

It was time for her to leave. Slipping the vial back into the sack at her side, she glanced at the stranger one more time. His face looked innocent, and his eyes seemed kind—at least they had in the brief moment she had seen them under the water.

"I'm glad you're alive," she whispered. "We are close enough to the shipwreck, so I'm sure a search party will find you here soon."

She stood, quickly glancing around her.

Before she had properly checked her back, two hands grabbed her by the shoulders.

"I got her!" a man's voice called out.

"Don't let her—" a woman's voice started to respond, but Aizel had already opened her mouth and started a song.

The song that came to mind was the song she used to fall asleep. It was not the smartest choice, but she did not have time to think of another. Maybe if she sang it loud enough, she could send these two and any others into a deep sleep.

That was all she would need to dash away.

Her words were cut short almost instantly by a hand clamping over her mouth.

"She's one of them, alright," the man's voice said from behind her.

". . . use her voice," the woman finished.

CHAPTER 7

*A*izel struggled against her captors, fighting to breathe through the large hand that remained clamped around her mouth.

"Stop that." The man shook her. "You aren't getting away, and you don't have your voice to save you."

Aizel ignored his frustrated command.

"Quit acting so scared." The woman stepped into Aizel's view. "She's not trained. She can't hurt you."

It took Aizel a moment to realize the woman was telling her captor not to be afraid of *her*.

"She's one of them," the man's voice continued. "It doesn't matter if she's trained. She's evil and powerful, and she's not wearing one of those spelled necklaces."

At the mention of the muting necklace, Aizel flung her head back in desperation. She made contact with the lower half of the man's face, and he temporarily loosened his grip.

Taking advantage of his shock, Aizel opened her mouth

and bit down hard on one of his chunky fingers. His skin tasted sour in her mouth, but she tried not to notice it.

He howled in pain but tightened his grip instead of loosening it.

"See?" he bellowed at his companion. "She is dangerous."

"She's unexpected," the woman countered. "Imagine how pleased they will be with us for finding one."

"But how are we going to get her back?" The man had pulled his hand from her teeth and tightened his arm around her neck, suffocating her instead of silencing her.

"Get . . ." Aizel gasped out the word as she clawed at his arm. She tried to repeat her head-butting success, but he managed to keep his skull safely out of her reach. "Get . . . off." She hissed out the words with the last of her breath.

"Just because we weren't prepared for this find doesn't mean we can't deal with it." The woman approached Aizel and shoved a bundle of twisted rope into her open mouth, effectively gagging her.

Aizel whipped her head back and forth to stop them from tying it, but she was no match against two people who were already holding her down.

The only good thing was that the man finally released his tight grip around her neck.

"You sure she can't do nothin' now?" he asked, moving to restrain her arms.

"Her magic is in her voice," the woman reassured. "Stop worrying. As long as she can't remove that, we'll be fine. Here, help me." The woman proceeded to bind Aizel's hands behind her back. "There. Are you through being afraid of a little girl now?"

"Oh, we did well." The man's voice was filled with glee.

He was seemingly unconcerned—or just hadn't noticed—that the woman was making fun of him.

"Yes, yes we did." The woman smiled. It wasn't a pleasant smile.

She appeared to be middle-aged, and her clothing was mostly brown and green with lots of leather straps and belts holding it in place. To Aizel, it appeared almost luxurious since it consisted of so many layers. But she had heard that everyone on the continent dressed this way. The woman seemed uncomfortably large as well. Not only was she tall but her body matched her bones, as though she had never missed a meal in her life.

Aizel had the sudden urge to slap the conniving, gleeful expression off the woman's face. She instinctively moved her arms to follow through on her desire, but the rope bit into her wrist.

No longer needing to hold her in place, the man stepped around her.

If Aizel thought the woman looked well-fed, she was shocked when she saw the size of the man. She had never seen anyone so tall or broad. She couldn't see a single bone on his body. He looked to be made purely of muscle.

It was unnerving. All the people she had ever known had sharp elbows and sallow cheeks.

She had always considered herself quite strong—swimming every day had given her a dense and wiry physique—but she was no match against these two.

"What about him?" the man asked, gesturing toward the stranger she had saved.

Looking at him now, Aizel wondered who he was. He was quite tall and had been difficult to lift and drag across the sand, but his body was more boyish compared to theirs. Perhaps not all Quotidian were as large and well fed.

"Leave him," the woman said. "If he's not gone already, he will be by the time the village organizes a rescue."

The man nodded but approached the stranger anyway.

The woman grabbed Aizel by the elbow and started dragging her down the beach. "Mingus, come."

Aizel jerked her arm out of the woman's grasp. Everything about the woman, especially her touch, made Aizel's skin crawl.

If only she hadn't helped the sinking man, she wouldn't be in this mess. If he had been conscious, he probably would have done exactly what these two were currently doing.

Rage and frustration exploded in Aizel's heart. She had come so far, only to be stopped when her feet touched the ground of freedom.

"Frisia," Mingus called. "I think this is the king's son who came in this morning. I saw him riding at the head of the reinforcements."

Frisia smiled once again. "Even better. We'll be sure to report that."

The king's son? All feeling left her body as Aizel thought she might be sick.

She had just saved the son of her worst enemy.

CHAPTER 8

*E*rich was dead. He had to be.

He could see nothing but reddish shadows.

Could taste nothing but salt.

Feel nothing but dryness. Heat. Pain.

He had never given much thought to death. His life philosophy was all about living. But if he'd had to guess what death felt like, this would be it. Except for the fact that he had not expected to be so thirsty in the afterlife.

"Here's another!" The voice sounded far away. Erich heard the words but could not comprehend what they meant.

His lips stung, his throat was parched, and his skin was burning on top and itching underneath. Every inhale felt like someone was stabbing his insides with a thousand little needlepoints.

Wait . . . A person wasn't supposed to breathe when they were dead.

He felt a hand on his head and, a moment later, a glorious trickle of cool water poured into his mouth.

Instinctively, he swallowed it. The water soothed his throat. He greedily lifted his head further from the ground so he could swallow better, and his hands reached forward to ensure the water poured faster.

"He's alive." The voice was closer this time.

Erich didn't feel alive. But he was thankful the water had cleansed the salty flavor from his lips, even if he could still feel it in the back of his throat.

Maybe he was alive.

His eyes burned. If he was alive, why was everything so dark?

Oh. Probably because he hadn't opened his eyes yet. He attempted to lift his eyelids, but it resulted in more burning pain.

Sitting up fully, he grabbed the waterskin someone was still holding to his mouth.

"Don't gulp it all down at once," a woman's voice admonished. It sounded strangely familiar.

He ignored her, focused as he was on getting his eyes open and free of pain. With a pang of regret, he poured some water on his hands instead of in his mouth. It was a shame to waste such delicious water.

Splashing it onto his eyes, he slowly rubbed them open.

He was sitting on a beach, which explained the dryness, sand, and sunburnt skin. His entire body was exhausted and aching, as though he were covered in bruises.

Someone was with him. His mind was slowly catching up to his body. Or was it the other way around?

Turning his head, he came face to face with someone he never thought he'd see again.

Her face was shadowed under a green hood, but he recognized her blue eyes instantly. It seemed she no longer had the face of the young girl he once knew, when she had been like an older sister to him. No, this powerful young woman, dressed in the tactical clothing of a woodsman, had a new confidence and edge about her.

Erich saw the moment she recognized him. He was a few years younger than she was, and he'd probably changed more significantly. But after taking in his face, she opened her eyes wide and softened her expression into the barest hint of a smile.

"Ro—" He started to say her name, but she quickly cut him off with a swift shake of her head.

"Will. John!" Two men stepped into Erich's peripheral vision. "Get him closer to the monastery to ensure he's found before he passes out again." She stood somewhere out of his sight. "Everyone else, continue combing the shoreline for survivors. They are clearly not looking this far out, which is probably intentional."

Erich twisted his head to watch her leave, but a shooting pain in his neck hampered the motion. He wasn't confused by her rejection, but he was sad to see her walk away. He wanted to know what she had been doing all these years—and how she had been.

"Thank you . . ." he attempted to call after her, but his voice came out in a quiet croak easily muted by the sound of the sea.

CHAPTER 9

Murky ocean water assaulted Erich's face. He could feel the cold wetness spread over his skin.

It pressed against his nose and mouth, forcing itself inside his body and taking control of him.

Erich batted his hands against it, trying to push it away or swim out of it. But the water was too sticky. It had become thick like tar, grabbing onto him and pulling him into it. The harder Erich fought, the stronger it gripped him.

The liquid in his nose and mouth solidified, blocking his breath and filling his throat. His mouth dried out, leaving his lips cracked and tasting of salt.

He was sinking, sinking, sinking, and he couldn't break free.

Erich jolted up.

His heart was pounding, his body covered in a layer of sweat.

He wasn't underwater.

Looking around, he tried to convince his brain that everything was fine.

He was in a bed in the old monastery the soldiers had taken over as their home base. Despite the previous day's attack, most of the interior of the sprawling stone building was still intact.

Unable to bear the thought of falling back into his nightmare, Erich stood and paced the small cell. The sky outside was still dark, and he was too disoriented to know what time of night it was.

He hadn't been scared during the shipwreck itself, but now he was terrified of repeating the experience.

Search parties were still combing the coastline and coming back mostly empty-handed. The thought made him furious. So many of his men—his father's men—had been murdered by the Majis.

Sleep was useless.

He slipped his captain's doublet over his loose woolen shirt, then stood and affixed the front clasps. He hated the dark gray uniformity of the Iseldis military. The shirt was designed to make its wearer look intimidating and powerful. Heavily layered bands of leather covered each shoulder, a series of knotted ties slanted down the left front, and a boldly embroidered insignia sat over his heart.

Finally, a small circlet of pure gold was sewn above the Iseldis insignia to mark him as a member of the royal family.

Erich loathed it.

When Ian wore the uniform, he looked older and more mature. People respected him, and he deserved it. The clothing accentuated who Ian really was.

For Erich, the gray shirt had always made him feel like he was playing a role, quieting some part of himself to fit in.

He especially hated how wearing the uniform made some of the guards act like they were more important than they were. They used it to intimidate others. Erich vowed he would never allow himself to become like that.

He had forced himself to accept the gray shirt as a mark of his station while resenting it ever so slightly whenever he had to put it on.

Walking through the halls of the once-peaceful monastery felt odd to Erich. It was now filled with soldiers and weapons.

The arched pathways overhead and domed rooms on either side stood tall and proud against the destructive sand-filled wind constantly rolling in from the sea. But when he looked closer, the crumbling masonry and deteriorating cracks of the structure gave it an air of exhaustion. This was the oldest known building in all of Iseldis, and perhaps even in all the Five Kingdoms. Throughout its entire history, it had housed the good monks, weathering them through storms and wars. Until now.

King Gareth and the Council in Chendas had asked the monks to leave the monastery a few months prior as the storms from the sea raged ever more dangerously. In return, Gareth had sent a contingent of his men to aid in the defense of the eastern shore. Currently, it was Gareth's general who was overseeing the monastery.

Walking through the long, silent hall, Erich felt a twinge of remorse. This had always been a place of peace. Though loyal to their king, the monks had never sided with any political power, choosing instead to rule their fields and community in their own fashion. It was said that even the Majis rulers of long ago had respected that.

Now, even in the middle of the night, the old monastery

was brimming with as much activity as it had during the day. Guardsmen and farmers from the local communities dashed through the maze of halls, delivering messages, repairing damages, and eating heartily between tasks.

A few of the elite guards who had come with Erich from the capital stopped and nodded respectfully as he passed.

Erich nodded back at the men he regarded as equals, wishing he could tear the small golden crown from his shirt. Most of the locals didn't know who he was, and he preferred to keep it that way.

Arriving at the center of the complex, Erich knocked on the door to what had once been the study of the abbot who oversaw the community of monks.

A towering squire held open the door of the study, and Erich entered. He nodded at the older general seated at the large desk inside.

"Your Highness." The general welcomed Erich without rising, his eyes tired and shadowed in the lamplight.

"I am merely a captain, General," Erich corrected him for the dozenth time since his arrival on the coast. The hardened old man insisted on deferring to Erich's royal title, but something about the way he did it grated on Erich's nerves.

General Gautho was twice his age and one of the most respected military men in the Five Kingdoms. Just like Ian, he naturally received—and deserved—the respect of everyone in the room.

Erich wanted to have that someday. It would be much nicer than patronizing heads dipping to his face and jokes of his youth and incompetence whispered behind his back.

"Couldn't sleep?" the general asked.

Erich's spine stiffened subconsciously. Did the man know he was having nightmares? "Simply staying alert. Any news?"

"Yes, actually," General Gautho responded. "Though it isn't good. A small rowboat was spotted up the northern shore. We think it carried the Majis who controlled the sea."

Erich crossed his arms. "A single magic-wielder turned the sea upside down?"

General Gautho shrugged. "This is what we are dealing with."

"What happened to the rowboat? Did it rejoin the main ship?"

"Surprisingly, no. The main ship left to avoid the aftermath of the wave. Mingus here saw the rowboat land."

Erich turned to the hulking man who stood by the door. "What happened to the Majis?"

"She disappeared into the woods," Mingus said. "I tried to follow her, but I was a long way off. By the time I got to the boat and the woods, I couldn't find her trail."

"Have we sent out a search party?" Erich whipped back around to face the general.

"Yes." He sighed, the shadows under his eyes seeming to grow twice as large. "But we have precious few men to send. We need every able body here in preparation for the next attack."

"We can't leave someone that powerful to freely roam our lands!" Erich did not attempt to hide his shock, though he did hope he'd masked his fear.

"I'm doing the smartest thing I can with the resources I have." The general's words were kind, but his tone was obviously meant to remind Erich that one of them was far more experienced than the other.

"Iseldis is grateful you are here," Erich said, speaking in the voice his father often used. "If you hadn't been here in time for this attack, the enemy could have easily taken over this shoreline entirely."

The general shook his head. "It isn't enough."

Erich guessed the man hadn't slept in the two nights since the attack. "I have some knowledge of tracking," Erich said. "As you do not need my help here personally, I could take on the mission of tracking this Majis."

The general looked up, his eyes shrewd. "This is a dangerous task, Your Highness."

Erich held his shoulders tall. "It is my kingdom she will be ravaging. This feels like the appropriate balance of responsibility. You remain here to aid in the defense of the whole continent, even though it is on Iseldis's shore. And I will traverse the lands I know well in search of the enemy." This was his chance to prove himself and ensure that justice was meted out, for his men and for his father.

The general nodded slowly.

Erich thought he saw a new flicker of respect in the older man's eyes.

"I don't have enough resources to refuse this generous offer," Gautho said. "You are sure you can take on this danger?"

"No," Erich responded honestly. "But no one is prepared for this."

"So be it," the general said. "Let me know how I can support you before you leave."

Erich nodded, then turned to the squire. "Can you tell me what this Majis looked like?"

The large man scrunched his face in thought, his mouth forming a round shape. "She was some distance away." He pointed at the stone wall of the study as if he could still see her. "She was dressed all in . . ." His forehead creased even more, and he closed his eyes. "Brown. Sandy brown, like the sand. I didn't get a good look at her face, but her hair was on fire."

"What?" Erich had been committing the man's every word to memory, but his last comment made no sense. "She was on fire? Perhaps she was not the Majis, but a poor villager who had been hit by the fireball attack from the larger ship."

"No." Mingus had opened his eyes, and his whole expression went wide as well. "She was glowing. It wasn't actual fire, see, it was just . . . her hair."

Erich did not see. "Her hair was glowing?"

Mingus nodded solemnly. "With fire." He shuddered slightly. "She's a powerful sorceress, that one."

Erich needed no convincing of that. "Thank you, Mingus."

The man nodded, glancing toward the general for his next orders. General Gautho waved his hand in dismissal, and Mingus stepped back to his post by the door.

CHAPTER 10

*A*izel slipped off her horse, clinging to the mare's mane in an attempt to support her exhausted legs.

After taking her to a building on the coast, the Quotidian soldiers had held her in a small pantry-like room. It was partially underground but had broken shelves lining the walls and remnants of dried herbs hanging from the low ceiling beams. They had also taken away her one small sack of supplies. Hopefully, her mother wouldn't be too disappointed about losing the small heirloom bottle—if Aizel ever saw her again.

Rather than put her immediately on a ship headed back to Istroya, however, the Quotidian soldiers had brought her inland. No one had told her where they were going, and she had no voice with which to ask them. Their journey had taken a fortnight and, despite their official-looking uniforms, the soldiers had only traveled with her under the cover of darkness.

She had never ridden a horse before—they were in scant

supply on Istroya—and endless hours in the saddle hadn't been kind to her.

Aizel had waited for an opportunity to escape, but she hadn't gotten a chance. Her jaw hurt from the rope gag, and her muscles ached from the unfamiliar gait of the horse.

It appeared they had arrived at their destination. Not that it was a comforting thought. From what she could tell, they were in the courtyard of a central palace in a large city. After they had kept to what seemed like small side roads during the entirety of their nightly journey, this was easily the most densely populated place she had seen on all of the continent. Even at this dark hour of the early morn, the city teemed with light and life.

An old man with a long, thin, white beard approached the captain of the men who had escorted her here.

"Is His Majesty ready for us now?" the captain asked. He and his four companions had not spoken a single word to Aizel during their travels.

"His Majesty is always ready. Come quickly." The old man disappeared as quickly as he had come.

The captain used his head to gesture toward Aizel. Two of the soldiers—whom she referred to as Sweaty and Stench in her head—approached her.

She released her tight grip on the horse's mane, glad that her legs seemed somewhat stable, and stepped toward the captain before they could lay a hand on her. The only freedom she had left was her dignity, and she took advantage of it as often as possible.

As they climbed the steps of the palace, Aizel was awed by the monolithic structure. She had never seen anything as tall as this building, even though they appeared to be entering it from the back. She could not imagine how much more magnificent the front would be.

The entire palace looked to have been carved out of a single slab of white marble. She could not fathom how that would have been possible, unless it had once been a cliff or mountain composed entirely of the snowy white rock.

Even in the dark of night, the marble easily reflected light from both the night sky above and the torches and firelight of the city below. It literally glowed. If she hadn't been so skeptical of what she would find inside, the sight would have been pure beauty. Nothing she had ever seen in her life could compare to the cold magnificence of the building looming above her.

She had no time to stare, unless she wanted the aid of Sweaty and Stench, so she hurried after the captain. A short web of unnecessarily tall hallways brought them to a closed door.

The bearded man stood outside it, tapping his finger against his arm. As soon as they stepped into view, he leaped into action and opened the door.

Just before they passed through it, he held out his pointer finger. "Remove that. His Majesty does not like to see it." He pointed at the rope gag in Aizel's mouth.

"Are you sure that is wise?" The captain's face seemed a touch flushed. It was the first time Aizel had seen him lose his unflappable exterior.

"We have several mages in the room who can counteract her if she attempts anything." The old man smiled behind his beard as he made eye contact with Aizel. His smile seemed like a challenge, as if daring her to make a move against them.

Sweaty and Stench stepped forward to untie the rope

behind her head. As they swung the annoying thing from her mouth, she loosened her sore jaw, exhaling in a light hiss.

To her satisfaction, Sweaty and Stench started in alarm, and even the captain blanched for a moment.

The bearded man did not so much as blink. "Your voice remains silent," he stated, not even bothering to tack a threat onto the end of his words.

It felt odd to be such an anomaly here. None of the taskers on Istroya worried about whether a Majis was muted or not because they could all wield magic as well. Painful magic.

However, that did not seem to be the case here. She folded that thought into her mind to mull over later.

For now, she needed to pay attention. She was about to meet her greatest enemy.

She followed the captain through the doorway.

The room was small but still held half a dozen people. Its ceiling was so high overhead that Aizel wondered whether it was the same height as the castle's exterior. The room felt like the inverse of a tall column. The only chair it contained was a similarly tall throne, carved out of the same white marble and positioned atop a raised stone dais.

Next to the throne stood a middle-aged man, his arms crossed and his feet in a wide stance. The bearded man who had greeted them hopped up the dais steps with surprising alacrity and stood on the other side of the throne.

As the men around her stopped to make obeisance to their king, Aizel stepped forward unattended to the center of the room. She stood tall and confident, staring straight at the only seated person there.

Every rule, decree, and retribution on Istroya was carried out under this man's name. She had hated and feared him her whole life. When she had escaped the island, her goal was to free herself from his influence—not land herself directly under it.

She had spent hours dreaming of obscenities to yell at him were she ever to meet him face to face, but her mouth was dry. She swallowed uncomfortably. The least she could do was show him she wasn't cowed by him, so she kept her back as straight as possible and stared up at his focused eyes.

His face held none of the glee or cruelty she had always imagined. In fact, he was far younger than Aizel had expected him to be. He appeared only a few years older than herself. Despite the bulky layers of clothing he wore and the tall height of his throne, she thought he looked rather small. He was probably shorter than everyone else in the room, except for her.

"*Another* prisoner, Turio?" the young king asked, his head resting lazily against his fist.

The disinterest in his voice fueled Aizel's fury. She was not *another* prisoner, another diver, another number. It was almost comical. The longer she was treated as such, the more she loathed it. One would think she'd be used to it by now.

"This is the escaped diver, Your Majesty." The older man, whose name must be Turio, leaned forward as he spoke, causing his long, thinning beard to sway stiffly.

The king raised his eyebrows just the smallest fraction, but Aizel could feel the energy of the room changing instantly.

He was interested in her, and that gave *her* power.

The bearded man had not noticed the king's subtle change of interest and had continued speaking into his monarch's ear. "This is the same sorceress who upset your plans at the seaside attack some time ago."

The young king nodded without turning his face to Turio.

Aizel kept her eyes glued to his from her place below the throne's dais. She had upset their plans? She had no idea what she had done, but she was suddenly quite proud of herself.

The king merely stared at her as everyone in the room waited silently.

"She is dangerous, Your Majesty." The wide-legged man opposite Turio leaned down to speak directly in the king's ear, but his whispered words were loud enough for the whole room to hear.

Aizel caught a flicker of annoyance on the king's face as he lifted his head and waved the man away. "I know her power."

Though the king's voice was neither angry nor dismissive, the older man jolted back as if he had been reprimanded.

"Do not fear, Younn," the king continued. "She shall make up for the disruption to our plans."

Aizel swallowed but kept her face passive. She had seen what the taskers did to other Majis who'd been caught trying to escape.

Turio smiled, the grim gesture visible behind his thinning facial hair. "What did you have planned, Your Majesty?"

"She shall repair what she has damaged," the king said simply, as though that explained everything.

Aizel focused on the small bit of power she still had in this exchange. She did not know why the young king was interested in her, but she would rather die than aid him. Literally. Her thoughts raced, but she kept them to herself.

Then, with a small smile, she realized her mouth was free.

She could say whatever she wanted. "I would rather die than help you," Aizel said, speaking for the first time in multiple days.

Two guards at the side of the room instantly raised their hands, fingers spread wide as their palms reached high.

Aizel tried not to visibly flinch. The taskers could cause horrible pain by merely lifting their hands, using their magic to amplify any chaos within their intended victim.

The king raised his hand to stop them.

For the first time since she had entered the room, his clean-shaven face twisted into a smile. "But would you let your sister die in your place?"

CHAPTER 11

"You look awful." Prince August of Allys raised his eyebrows at Erich.

"I feel awful," Erich replied. He had been traveling for nearly a month's time in search of the Majis sorceress. "Also, hello to you, too," he continued sarcastically. "So good to see you after all this time."

"And here I thought we were close enough friends to skip through the falsehoods and speak right to the heart of the matter." August shrugged, a warm smile on his welcoming face.

Erich grinned back at him. "I am honestly sure you're so thrilled to see me that you don't care I am unannounced."

"It's good to see you again, friend, unexpected as it is," August said. "What can I do for you?"

Erich's shoulders dropped. "We have much to cover. But important things first. Could I trouble you for a bath and a bed to stay the night?"

"I've already called for a bath. I could smell you from the courtyard."

Erich narrowed his eyes. "Now I remember why I have not visited you for so long, friend."

August merely grinned as he led the way deeper into the castle. "You found your brother?"

"Aden? Yes. He's been hiding out in a villa here in your impassable mountains. He's been doing quite well, actually, despite the effects of this beast-like curse." Erich did not mention the additional information his brother had given him. Aden had his human faculties despite the beastly body, but the curse would soon claim his body and mind.

Erich kept his exterior lighthearted as he bantered with his friend, but a bright rage continued to burn deep inside him. His brother had attempted to stay positive, especially in the presence of the young noblewoman who had befriended him.

But Erich could sense Aden's deep sadness, and it tore him apart. How was he supposed to make his brother feel better in the face of such a devastating fate? He had done his best to make Aden smile, but again he had felt so useless.

So, he had funneled that feeling into anger. Anger at the cruel Majis sorcerer who had cursed his brother. Anger at the capricious Majis sorceress who had doomed his men to a watery death.

"Have you heard any news of the sorceress I am tracking?" Erich asked, his mind returning to his main objective.

"She was seen in a small village a day's ride south of here," August replied.

Erich stopped walking and grabbed his friend's shoulder. "Are you sure? I have not heard any solid news in some time.

I should leave immediately." Erich turned back toward the direction they had come.

"No need to rush off." August stopped him. "Let me explain it further. She was seen nine days ago, so if she left any trail, it is already cold. Stay here tonight and rest. Again, you look like you could use it." He smiled cheekily.

Erich's expression relaxed. August's attempt at humor during this stressful time was a welcome distraction. His body begged for a night of rest in the sprawling, sunlit castle of Allys rather than under bushes or in cramped tavern rooms.

He hadn't been lying to General Gautho that he had some skill in tracking, but that didn't mean he enjoyed it.

Left alone in a luxurious guest room, Erich immediately sat down to unlace his boots. While the worn leather felt like a second skin, his feet begged for freedom. The creamy sandstone walls and warm red furnishings lifted his mood instantly, but the steaming copper tub beside the bed did quite the opposite.

Approaching it, Erich stepped into the warm water with a single bared foot. While the sensation was relaxing, it also caused his heart to race. The water barely covered his ankle, but it felt oppressively heavy, as if it would crush him.

His lungs began to struggle for air, though he was merely standing in the tub and had not even fully removed his clothing.

Why did the water feel so suffocating?

A cold sweat broke out across Erich's neck and shoulders, and he felt his legs go weak.

If his legs truly gave out, he would collapse into the water.

He quickly jumped out of the tub.

This was ridiculous. He was having a nightmare and he wasn't even sleeping.

Giving in to his shaking body, he sat back on the bed. This was not him. He was not like this. He was Erich Sirilian, the happy, confident prince who made every time a fun time.

How could he be the envy of everyone in the room if he couldn't even take a bath to wash the stench of the road from his body?

Grabbing a towel, he dipped a corner of it in the hot tub. After wringing out the excess water, he buried his face in the warm, wet cloth. He did not have to immerse himself in water to be clean.

As his body finally relaxed, his mind clung to his current mission. It was beyond frustrating to have spent so long searching for this dangerous woman only to continually come up empty-handed.

His only consolation was—at least as far as they were aware—she had not yet made an attack. Erich hoped the constant pressure of having him right on her tail had forced her to check her power.

It was not much of a consolation, though. The Majis had to be stopped.

"Prince Erich?" A knock sounded at the door.

Erich lifted his head. "Yes?"

"A report just arrived from Iseldis. The sorceress has been found and secured. She is being held at the old monastery. General Gautho has requested your presence as soon as possible."

Erich jumped from the bed. Getting rest would have to wait, but at least he was mostly clean.

CHAPTER 12

$\mathcal{A}$izel watched in horror as a guard led her sister into the room through a door on the opposite side.

Celesta looked confused but otherwise unharmed. She was wearing a white ribbon snug around her neck. A small jewel was attached to it. The sight of the hated device gave Aizel a small moment of relief.

If they had silenced her sister, they hadn't yet discovered she could not speak.

When Celesta saw Aizel, her face lit up in disbelief and she leapt forward, throwing herself into her sister's arms.

Aizel hugged Celesta tightly as her heart pounded. She would do anything to get her sister out of this place.

Celesta pulled back, her face twisted into a frown as she poked Aizel in the chest. She rapidly made small movements with her hand, pointing at Aizel, slicing through the air with a flattened hand, and then pointing to herself. *"You left me."*

Aizel nodded, her eyes downcast. *"I'm sorry."* It was not uncommon for Majis to speak to each other with their hands on Istroya, so Aizel was not worried that their method of communication would reveal Celesta's secret.

Celesta pointed to herself and then Aizel, then slashed her hand across her face. *I thought you were dead.*

Aizel nodded. "I know," she mouthed. "I'm sorry. I was trying to save you."

"I always wished I had a brother," the king's voice cut into their silent conversation.

Aizel pulled Celesta close, keeping her sister's face angled away from the king so she couldn't read his lips.

"Or a sister would have been fine as well," he continued. "Someone to share the joys and sorrows of life. A friend. Someone to confide in." His face was pensive, as if he had the wisdom one only gained in old age. "But I was never given that gift. Instead, I was given a broken kingdom and some weak alliances, along with the mandate to unite them all. To make it the true place for all people to live in contentment rather than constant fear."

Celesta had tried to turn in Aizel's arms to see the king and find out what was going on, but Aizel gently twisted her back, burying her younger sister's face in a hug.

"What does that have to do with my sister?" Aizel's mind was too full to follow along with his word games.

"You want what is best for your sister?" the king asked.

Aizel did not deign to give him a response.

Not seeming bothered by that, he continued, "Imagine feeling that sense of responsibility for every living soul on this continent. I do not have a sister, sorceress, but I do know how you feel. We are alike, you and I."

Aizel shook her head. She was nothing like this young king, and she would never admit it.

"One day you will see it more clearly." Again, he seemed relatively unbothered by her direct opposition.

"Now, imagine someone took your little sister, the one you love so much, and did something that put her in harm's way?"

Aizel did not have to imagine very hard to understand how that would feel.

"I am doing everything in my power to make life better for those I am responsible for. They are living in fear. And your actions have upset those plans, hurting my little brothers and sisters." His voice was both sorrowful and accusing as he looked down at her from his throne.

Aizel stared back at him, confused. Had it not been his Quotidian soldiers who had caused the giant wave, destroying at least one ship full of men and dealing damage all along the coast? Or was there some other Quotidian faction he was working against?

"You see . . ." His face softened into a smile. "We do understand each other quite well, do we not?"

"My sister?" Aizel lost her carefully composed façade. "What does my sister have to do with any of this?"

"Justice begs for fulfillment," the king said. "You have wronged me by taking something I want."

"I don't understand," Aizel said, eager to keep the conversation away from Celesta. The only thing she had done was to stop collecting pearls for him and his taskers. "You had no idea I existed until a short time ago. Will you actually miss the work of a single diver?"

"No." The king shook his head. "You saved a life I was trying to destroy. You took my well-laid plan and rendered it useless."

Aizel narrowed her gaze. He was speaking of the prince she had saved from the sea.

But this boy king was far too young to be a father, which meant the prince she had saved was the son of a different king on the continent.

"So now," the king continued with a smile, "I have something you want, and you will give me something I want."

Aizel was struggling to follow his logic, if indeed one could call it logic. It was also getting harder to keep her sister from turning toward the king before he revealed his true intentions. "You're bluffing."

The king shook his head, the smile on his face spreading to a broad grin as though he were enjoying this conversation immensely. He glanced back at Turio. "She thinks I'm bluffing."

As soon as he saw the king's expression, the old man burst out laughing. "She thinks you're bluffing."

The king's face became serious again as he shifted his gaze back to Aizel.

Noting the change in the king's mood, Turio immediately stopped laughing. "His Majesty never bluffs."

"What do you want?" Aizel glanced between the king and his advisor, trying to follow the balance of power.

"I want the life of a son of Frederich of Iseldis. You take a life, and I will free a life. It is poetic justice." The king's face turned thoughtful. "And it is in my power to give you this opportunity."

His request was both easier and more difficult than Aizel had expected. She had never killed someone before, and she did not relish the thought of doing so. But in exchange for Celesta's life . . . she couldn't just say no. "How many sons does King Frederich have?" she asked, stalling for time.

The king flicked his hand toward the other man standing near the throne.

"Four," the man answered.

"He will hardly miss one," the king added. "Though he might miss them all should something happen to each of them." The small smile on the king's face told Aizel that he dearly hoped something would indeed happen to each of them.

"Does it matter which one I . . . dies?" Aizel asked, unable to even kill someone in a sentence.

The king shook his head. "No, but I shall provide you with an easy opportunity to take the life of the one you saved." He smiled, seemingly pleased with himself.

Aizel had an astonishing realization. "Was that entire attack just to rid yourself of one man?"

The king shrugged. "Among other things, yes."

Aizel was intrigued. The enemy of her enemy was her . . . friend? "Why is it so important that he die?"

"I would not expect you to understand."

Aizel felt like the king was speaking to her as he would to a small child. "Try me."

"I am," he responded, still smiling serenely. "I am giving you the chance to save your sister's life by providing something I want."

"The death of your enemy?"

"Yes." The king tapped the arm of his throne, finally growing impatient.

Aizel knew her questions sounded obvious, but she had just intentionally forced the king to admit that this Frederich of Iseldis—or at least one of his sons—was his enemy.

"Do we have a deal?" he asked.

"What happens to me if I succeed in killing this prince?"

she asked, realizing that the end of the bargain hadn't been mentioned.

"That depends on how well you succeed," the boy king responded. "I am a just king. As such, I can assure you that, if you do not return here having fulfilled this request, your sister will die."

Aizel nodded. "But you will not harm her—she is safe in your justice—until I return?"

The king nodded. "You'd best see that you return."

Aizel shivered at his threat. She could only hope that he would be honest in keeping Celesta safe until then. Her grip tightened possessively on her little sister before Celesta finally managed to push herself away and glance through the room.

Seemingly satisfied, the king flicked his fingers.

Two guards from the back of the room approached her from behind and lifted a ribbon to her neck.

Instantly recognizing the device, Aizel sprang out of reach, holding out her hands in defense. "That was not in the bargain."

"I can't have a Majis running free around my country-side," the king said.

"But how shall I defend myself if this prince tries to kill me first?" Aizel asked, once again stalling for time.

"My dear girl, your life matters nothing to me. If you want your sister to live, you will carry out this task—without using your magic or further disrupting my plans—and return here to prove it."

Aizel was done being silenced. "Your Majesty, my sister's life is threat enough. I love her more than anyone or anything in my life. I would do anything for her. I have been before you this whole time without trying to use my magic. I can promise you that I will not use it again while her life is in danger."

The king stood, flicking his hand at the back guards. "Of course you did not try to use it here in front of my mage guards. They would have stunned you in moments. They almost did the first time you stupidly opened your mouth. How naive do you think I am? Now shut your mouth. Turio, arrange the rest."

Without another glance in her direction, the king left the room.

"No! Please—" Aizel attempted to block the guards, but within seconds they had tied the ribbon around her throat and cut off her plea.

A familiar weight settled at the base of her neck, making it difficult to breathe.

Reaching up, she fingered the single malachite gemstone that hung from the soft white ribbon. Tears stung at her eyelids.

I will come back for you soon, she signed to Celesta as Sweaty and Stench grabbed her upper arms and yanked her toward the side door.

CHAPTER 13

They left the marble palace the following morning. Traveling back to the coast took another fortnight. At least this time she had free movement of her hands since Turio—who had come with them—convinced the soldiers she could not remove the muting necklace on her own.

Which was true. She couldn't.

Aizel's entire body reacted with longing when they crested a hill and she saw the sea stretching out below. She had not realized how calming—and cleansing—it was to swim daily. No wonder Sweaty and Stench were, well, sweaty and stenchy. Her body felt hidden under an extra layer of grime and dirt from their traveling, and her brown underdress seemed to have turned a new, darker shade of brown.

If the five men escorting her had noticed that she was beginning to smell as horribly as they did, they hadn't said anything or offered her an opportunity to bathe.

Perhaps they simply hadn't noticed. They tended to stay as far from her as possible while still ensuring she was constantly guarded.

For the most part, she appreciated their distance, but being treated with such fear and disdain was beginning to take a toll on her.

Turio was the only one who did not seem to be affected by her presence. Although she hadn't seen the old man use magic, she assumed he could—at least, based on the way the others were treating her.

The Quotidian men who couldn't use magic were the ones who treated her like she was some kind of monster.

She had no opportunity to even get near the sea as they immediately returned to the ancient stone building from which they had started this whole journey.

Shortly afterward, she found herself back in the small half-underground pantry room. As it was still dark, she could see very little of the room around her. But she gratefully sank onto the soft sandy floor, hugging her knees for warmth.

For the first time in several days, she was indoors and alone.

Her eyes slowly closed, and she gave in to the exhaustion until the jiggling lock outside the door brought her back to consciousness.

The early morning light streamed through the high, barred window above her head, illuminating the door as it pushed inward.

The hulking man who had found her on the beach—Minkus?—stood in the doorway.

Aizel scrambled to her feet, pressing her back into the wall behind her.

But the giant of a man merely sneered at her, crossing his arms as he stepped aside to allow Turio entrance.

Aizel crossed her arms. Turio's half-smile was more chilling than the light breeze coming in through the open-air window.

"Take this," he said, tossing her a small fabric sack.

Catching it out of the air, she recognized it as the pillow she'd brought from home. She opened it, scanning the interior. Everything was there except for her mother's vial.

"Looking for this?" Turio held out his other hand, opening it to reveal the pearlescent bottle.

Aizel looked from the bottle to his face. Surely, he wanted something else from her or he would not have withheld the vial to begin with.

He held her gaze for a moment, then tossed the bottle to her.

She caught it before it crashed to the ground. Clutching it to her chest for a moment, she regained her composure and then used her thumb to gently nudge the metal lid open.

The sweet aroma of the lotus oil instantly hit her nose. She raised the bottle higher to inhale the familiar scent. She wasn't sure why he was returning it to her, but she relished the small piece of home.

"The prince should arrive later today," Turio said. "He will be escorting you back to Chendas. You will carry out your task and report back to the marble palace. No one can know you are working on behalf of the great king, or your sister dies." Turio's face was far too happy to be making such a statement.

Aizel inhaled, knowing she would have to see this horrible thing through. For someone who appeared so weak,

Turio was more calculatedly cruel than any of the brutish taskers Aizel had ever known.

"You must also bring proof that Erich is dead." The white beard continued to wag stiffly under the old man's mouth. "I have prepared all the particulars for today. Everything else should go quite simply for you." He sounded as though he expected her to thank him.

Quite simply? Aizel wanted to ask, the words stopping in her throat. *What about this is simple? Why does the prince have to die? What threat does he pose to the king? And how am I supposed to actually . . . you know, do the thing?*

"Excellent. No questions?" Turio asked.

She definitely had questions. Aizel reached up, pointing to the ribbon around her neck as she glared at the old man.

Turio smiled. Somehow, it made his expression harder instead of softer. "You wish to speak? I hardly think your voice could add anything to this conversation. It is much better if you simply listen."

Minkus—no Mingus, that was his name—scoffed from his place in the doorway.

Aizel did not think Turio was funny in the slightest. She opened the cloth sack and carefully placed the vial inside.

"I wish you luck," Turio said.

Aizel glared at him. She doubted that.

"No, really, I genuinely hope you succeed."

Why? Why are you going to such great lengths to kill this young man? She yelled her frustration in her head.

He turned to leave, and Mingus stepped away from the doorway. "Oh, wait." Turio stopped moving. "I forgot to mention something. That old vial? I added a few drops of poison to the perfume inside. That should come in handy, I would expect. No . . ." He looked over his shoulder, holding up his hand. ". . . need to thank me."

Aizel stared back at him in horror. She had just inhaled the scent of the vial. Would the poison affect her because of that? If she had wanted to bathe before, she felt filthy now.

As the door closed behind Turio and Mingus, Aizel sank back to the ground. She wanted to open her sack and examine the vial, but she was too afraid to touch it.

Perhaps it would make her job easier, but the thought sickened instead of soothed her.

She was beginning to feel sorry for this Quotidian prince who had no idea what he was up against. She would not wish Turio upon her worst enemy.

She tried to remember the stranger she had saved from the sea. In the brief moment his eyes had been open underwater, they had seemed honest and perhaps even kind. But he had been begging her to help him. Of course he had been honestly begging!

If only she could befriend the Quotidian prince and work with him against their mutual enemy.

After traveling back to the monastery in record time, Erich felt surprisingly calm at the sight of the ocean. With his newfound reaction to water, he was afraid the sight of the sea itself would cause him to go into a waking panic. But the waves crashing over the beach below the monastery did nothing more than provide a tranquil background sound.

It had been nearly six weeks since he had left the monastery, and his nightmares had continued almost every night. Perhaps they would cease, now that he had been able to see the ocean again without fear.

Riding into the courtyard, he was immediately greeted by General Gautho and a newly arrived councilor from Chendas. They must have received news of his arrival. The councilor was a tall man, old and wiry in both body and facial hair. Erich thought he recognized him from previous trips to Iseldis, but he couldn't place the man's name.

"Thank you for your haste, Captain," General Gautho

said. "Your diligent search took a great weight off my shoulders."

Erich felt his chest fill with pride at the older man's praise. "Where was she apprehended?"

"Near the sea not far from here," Gautho answered. "My patrol came across her while she was sleeping and was able to overpower her quite easily."

Erich nodded, wanting to move the conversation in a new direction—one that didn't dwell on the fact that he had essentially failed his month-long search despite the general's appreciation of it.

"Since she was apprehended on Iseldis's land," the councilor explained as General Gautho led them through the monastery, "she is under your jurisdiction. Hence the reason a representative of King Frederich—yourself—was summoned here along with myself."

Erich nodded. He had dispatched messengers to his father before leaving Allys to decide how to proceed with the matter. The sorceress was technically a prisoner of the kingdom of Iseldis, but only Chendas had the necessary knowledge for dealing with the Majis.

"King Gareth has offered to hold her in Chendas if Iseldis does not have the means of doing so," the councilor continued, as if reading Erich's mind.

"I received a message from my father this morning," Erich responded. "He agrees that she should be sent to Chendas. The Council will have a better understanding of how she can be safely removed from the upcoming war."

Erich had not yet decided if he was in agreement with his father. Only one of them had been on the sea that day, witnessing the vast amount of destruction she had wrought

—not only against the ship and its sailors, but also all along the coastline where the massive overflow of water had flooded into villages, homes, and farms. This one person had crippled them in a single day. Erich wanted justice. Justice for his people, justice for his month-long search, and justice for his repeating nightmares.

"I will escort her to Chendas myself," he added. Perhaps if he saw the matter through to the end, he would find peace.

General Gautho stopped walking and turned back to Erich. He seemed to have aged five years in the four weeks since Erich had seen him last, but his expression looked more relieved and respectful than Erich had ever seen. "Frankly, Captain, I am thankful to hear you say it. This woman is dangerous, and she must be our singular priority until she is safely under the care of the examiners. They will be able to keep her harmful magic away from our homes and families. In the best scenario, they may even find a way for her to turn the tides of this war in our direction. She might be our miracle."

Ahead of them, the hulking Mingus swung open a heavy wooden door, revealing a staircase that led into an undercroft.

The councilor stopped right at the top. "I appreciate your enthusiasm for this offer, General, but if I may speak plainly?"

"What is on your mind?" Gautho asked.

"The prince is young," the councilor continued, speaking slowly in a diplomatic voice. "Yes, he is a son of the renowned King Frederich, but is he truly up for a task such as this? This sorceress is cunning. She evaded his capture for days. And she is beautiful, an enchantress, a seductress.

Dealing with her will be entirely different than dealing with a violent warrior. Her tactics will be far more . . . manipulative." The councilor turned to Erich. "No offense at all toward Your Highness, of course."

"Of course," Erich responded, smiling over clenched teeth. He felt insignificant in front of this frail old man who had likely never lifted a sword in his life. "However, Councilor, I was here with the general during the last attack, and I saw my boat crushed to splinters in the jaws of the sea itself. I have seen the evil this sorceress commands, and I am under no illusion as to what we are dealing with here."

"The prince carried himself with remarkable maturity during that difficult time," General Gautho said.

Despite the hardened man's lack of emotion, Erich once again felt humbled by his affirmative words.

"As you say, General. I do not doubt you." The councilor handed a folded parchment to Erich. "You will need to sign this. I shall accompany you back to Chendas, of course."

Erich opened the document, scanning it quickly as he mumbled the words aloud.

Transfer of Political Prisoner from Iseldis to Chendas

Majis Sorceress Aizel—

Erich frowned, stumbling over the unfamiliar name. "Azel," he repeated to himself. "Like hazel." Continuing on, he read through the rest of the document.

—accused of leaving the Isle of Exile and instigating sea storms along the eastern coastline.

Highest danger level.

Though he had read these standard reports several times, Erich still felt his stomach tighten at the danger level warning.

The councilor and general had started down the steps that had been carved out of the sandstone earth, so he folded the parchment and followed them. He would sign it when he delivered the sorceress—Azel, a name he had never heard before—to the Council.

He glared at the back of the councilor's head, thinking that the wispy man was more likely to slow them down than aid them in any way. He looked as though his thin, white beard would simply deteriorate in the wind.

Erich held back his smirk. Now was not the time to be making jests. "Your knowledge would be most welcome," he said instead, wishing his father were present to witness his incredible amount of self-restraint. "Would you be able to spare a few guards to help escort this sorceress?" Erich asked General Gautho.

"Sadly, I do not know that I have anyone to spare," Gautho replied. "I will have to rely upon your skill once again."

Erich pursed his lips but did not complain. The coast was still their most vulnerable position, and they were under-manned as it was.

The expansive underground cellar was lit surprisingly well by short windows placed high along the upper perimeter of the wall. Giant barrels, large enough for a man to comfortably climb inside, littered the floor. Erich could smell the yeasty aroma of fermenting ale, though all the barrels appeared to be empty. Other items were strewn across the floor and the broken shelves lining the room. Everything was damp.

The sound of a loud rumbling came through the barred open-air windows.

Panic filled Erich; he flinched, unable to stop himself. The thunderous noise sounded exactly like the first crashing of the giant wave from the attack. "What's that?"

"Watch out!" the general yelled at the same time, moving quickly to the western wall—the wall farthest away from the ocean.

Erich followed the general's movements, although his stomach turned. He thought he might be sick right here in front of these two men. He did have enough presence of mind to grab the older councilor and pull him toward the far wall, shielding him from the unknown sound with his own body.

Seawater flooded through the upper windows, crashing onto the floor and splashing off the large barrels.

It swirled around the floor, but then the deluge stopped.

Although it was over in a matter of seconds, Erich's heart felt as though it were pounding in his throat. Backed up against the far wall, they had avoided getting drenched, but Erich shook himself nonetheless. Even the light spray of droplets that had hit him caused his neck and spine to tingle uncomfortably.

"What was that?" he asked, his voice awkwardly high.

"The sea has been even more fragile since the previous attack," General Gautho responded, wading back toward the center of the room. "We get some flooders every few days now. Nothing as intense as the one you witnessed, just some small reminders that they are out there and watching." The general's lack of sleep made more sense now.

"It's a good thing the monks got out of here in time," Erich commented, forcing confidence into the squeaking sound of his voice. It was a pity the Council had asked the monks to leave several months prior, but Erich could see why living here permanently was no longer safe.

"It's only too bad that all the ale they left behind was raided immediately. Would have been nice to find some full barrels here when we arrived." Gautho's voice was completely serious.

"If I were a thief, I'd have gone for the good stuff, too." Erich forced a tinny laugh.

The councilor smiled politely but did not seem amused by either of their comments. "The prisoner, General?"

Gautho nodded and continued moving down the long cellar.

Erich's feet seemed glued to the floor. He did not feel comfortable moving any closer to the sea-facing windows. So much for his nightmares ceasing. Tonight's would probably be the worst one yet.

He was unable to lift his eyes from the swirling water that lapped at his ankles. It splashed across the stone floor before splattering away through a large iron grate fixed to the floor in the center of the room.

"I take it the drainage system was built for their ale-making process, not for transporting unwanted floodwaters," Erich commented, buying time for his cowardly feet.

"Aye," the general replied. "And the open-air windows as well. The best ale makers claim that continuous fresh air improves the fermentation process and creates a better flavor, although I've no idea why."

Erich shrugged, still hesitant to leave the safety of the far wall. "I've had their ale, and it is easily the best I've ever tasted."

"The prisoner, Your Highness?" The councilor was halfway across the room and had turned back to face Erich.

Erich nodded curtly, inwardly cursing the man's intolerance for humor. He suppressed his fear and waited until the councilor's back was once again turned. Lifting each leaden foot, he slowly forced his way further into the underground room.

"This was the most secure place to keep her," the general said, pulling out a key to unlock a large wooden door.

He stepped aside so Erich could enter first.

The door opened to reveal a small pantry of ingredients for the monks' ale-making process. Wooden shelves lined every wall, though many of them were splintered, broken, and empty. This room also had a short, barred window at the highest point of the wall—which was still dripping from the recent flooder. A few sprigs of what had once been dried herbs were hanging from the window bars. They were very wet herbs now, dripping noisily upon the sandstone floor below them.

Erich's mind noticed all these things with the periphery of his vision, but his eyes remained trained on the true threat in the small old pantry.

The Majis sorceress stood in the center of the room, drenched in water. She, too, was still dripping from the recent wave.

Her arms hugged her sides, and her long, tangled hair was clumped around her face and shoulders. It was an indistinct brown that seemed to blend into the shapeless and torn brown tunic that clung to her tiny frame.

But it was her face that surprised him the most. This sorceress was barely more than a girl! She was probably Meena's age, if not younger. Her eyes remained unfocused, staring at the floor in front of her as if she hadn't even noticed the three men crowding into the small room.

She twitched her nose, scrunching it up in a way that distorted her whole face as her shoulders twitched as well.

"Ahhh . . . ahhh choo!" she sneezed.

Erich nearly burst out laughing. This small girl might be powerful enough to overturn the ocean, but he would not have to worry about her seducing him with her wiles.

She was a mess.

The mess inhaled with a sniffle, wiping her doubly wet nose on a baggy sleeve.

"Majis Sorceress Azel," Erich said, his voice deep and confident. "I am Captain Erich of the Iseldis elite guard, and I am here to transport you to the Kingdom of Chendas, where you will answer for your crimes against the good quotidian people of this continent."

Her eyes lifted to his face. She scanned it quickly as if looking for something, but when she didn't find it, she merely glared at him with an intensely focused hatred.

Erich couldn't care less about what she thought of him. He had been there when the ship had gone down, taking his men along with it. He knew what he thought of her, and he was ready to bring her—and her people—to justice.

She crossed her arms, making her body appear even smaller as she continued to glare at him.

When she said nothing in response, Erich turned to leave. He was anxious to get out of the wet cellar before another wave hit. "We leave at dawn. I hope you can ride a horse?"

She rolled her eyes, looking away, but said nothing.

"Then I also hope you are a quick learner." Erich turned to leave. Something about the whole scenario made him uncomfortable. She looked so innocent it unnerved him. "Rude little thing, isn't she?" Erich said to the general in an attempt to hide his own discomfort.

Gautho shrugged. "She's a Majis," he replied, as if that were reason enough to excuse any behavior.

Without a second glance at the pathetic girl who carried death and destruction in her wake, Erich left the room.

CHAPTER 15

*W*aiting in the monastery courtyard, Aizel shivered. She stared with growing unease at the three horses that were packed and ready for their journey, dreading the moment she would have to mount one of them.

Traveling by sunfish was vastly preferable.

The rude young prince stood across the courtyard, adding items to the saddlebags and giving orders to various Quotidian soldiers.

He hadn't glanced in her direction once, as though she were invisible or not even present.

Crossing her arms, she cradled her hands in the warmth of her armpits. The sun was working its way up the morning sky, offering the promise of a better temperature, but the long shadows were still cold.

Despite the early morning activity going on around her, Aizel felt alone. Every person passing through the courtyard gave her a wide berth.

They were ignoring her so thoroughly she felt tempted to jump onto the half wall next to her, throw herself on the nearest horse, and gallop out of the courtyard to freedom.

Would they even notice?

Of course they would. And then her sister's life would immediately be forfeit.

They were ignoring her because they knew she wasn't going anywhere.

And she knew she wasn't going anywhere.

She shivered, wishing the sun would rise more quickly. Or for someone to look her way and offer a spare cloak or blanket. Surely, they must have an extra layer of something here. If only she had her voice to ask for one. She sighed, but even that was devoid of sound. It came out simply as a heavy breath.

Her eyes wandered back to the prince. He was wearing a long-sleeved gray jacket. Its stiff shoulders seemed to contradict the open smile on his face as he chatted with one of the stable boys attending the large horses.

Yesterday, when he had sauntered into her pantry prison, he had been wearing colorful garb. Compared to everyone else she had seen here, it had made him look fresh and bright. For a moment, her heart had hoped he might truly be as different as his clothing suggested.

Then his cold, unfeeling eyes had roamed over her, landing on her face with disdain. He hadn't even deigned to judge her. He had simply looked down upon her and asserted his status as the superior Quotidian man.

Although she hadn't expected him to, she was disappointed he hadn't recognized her.

What Aizel had hoped for, however, was at least a touch of humanity from this ambiguous prince who was hated by her enemy. That assumption had been doused as well. So much for her slim hope of keeping him alive to aid her.

No, she was all alone here.

It was fine. She could handle alone.

However, watching the prince across the courtyard, she was briefly reminded of the vulnerable stranger she had found sinking in the sea. He was smiling as he talked, waving his arms in enthusiasm and patting the stable boy's shoulder. Not that he had looked like that when he'd been sinking. He'd just looked . . . more human.

As the stable boy turned to leave, Aizel could see a broad grin spreading across his face.

Meanwhile, the prince had turned his attention to a breathless woman who had just dashed out of the far building. She handed him a package wrapped in cloth.

Holding it up to his face, the prince groaned in happiness.

"It smells delicious," he told the woman, speaking so loudly his voice carried throughout the outside space. "It won't even feel like I'm traveling with food this good. Thank you."

He slipped the package into the saddlebags as the woman walked away, her step lighter and less frazzled.

It seemed everyone who walked away from the vibrant young prince was a happier person.

Aizel hugged herself tighter as she tried to remember the last time someone had smiled at her.

It was Turio. The last person who had smiled at her was Turio.

She shivered, turning her attention back to the horses to rid her mind of the image of Turio's parchment-pocked face.

Her stomach twisted. She didn't want to get back up on one of the tall, powerful animals.

Seemingly satisfied with the state of the saddlebags, the prince unhooked his horse's reins from the nearby post and held them in his hand, ready to mount and start their journey.

Aizel was not ready. Her heart had started to race as she tried to think of any way to get out of this situation.

She couldn't spend another two weeks shivering and miserable on the unsteady back of a tall, terrifying horse.

Nor could she envision herself opening the beautiful vial in her bag and slipping a drop into the prince's food.

No.

No.

No.

She would never be able to do it.

Her stomach was tight, her fingers and toes were cold, her head was light, and her knees were tingling.

She couldn't get back on that horse. And she couldn't kill another person, no matter how cold-heartedly they looked at her while smiling at everyone else.

She swallowed. The prince stood by his horse, petting the mare's long nose and whispering something into her ear. He wasn't terrified of horses. He even treated the animal with respect.

Maybe, just maybe, there was still hope. If she could somehow get through to him, she would be able to change his mind—about whatever it was he hated her for.

To start, she could try asking him a simple question, something that would be easy to communicate without her voice.

With a shaky breath inward, she took a step toward the prince.

Just then, Turio shuffled into the courtyard. "Were you

waiting on me, Your Highness?" he asked. "I am so sorry. These old bones do not like the sea air."

"Good morning, Councilor," the prince responded. "We are ready to be on our way as soon as you are." His words were kind, but Aizel could see the thinly veiled frustration behind them.

Interesting. The prince, who was kind to even a stable boy and a kitchen girl, could barely contain his dislike of Turio. That one realization eased a fraction of the tension in Aizel's stomach. At least they shared that in common. She moved toward him with more confidence in her step.

"Then let us be off," Turio proclaimed, approaching his own horse as two soldiers dashed forward to help him mount it.

The prince turned his back to Aizel, repositioning himself to mount his own steed.

Unable to call his name, she reached out and touched his arm.

He whirled around. For the briefest moment, he looked shocked as he stared down at her head.

Aizel wondered if something was in her hair and reached up to brush it away.

By the time her hand reached her head, he had quickly schooled his expression to the icy cold indifference he had shown yesterday. His eyes swept the length of her body and then drifted away, as if she were no more interesting than a rock on the side of the road.

A tight pain knotted at the base of her throat, just below the ribbon that circled her neck. She swallowed to release the pressure.

Lifting her hands, she crossed them over her shoulders, pretending to shiver as obviously as she could.

At least the motion caused him to return his attention to her, but his eyes narrowed in confusion. He leaned his head back, positioning his body ever so slightly away from her.

Ignoring the hollow feeling inside her chest, Aizel tried once more. Using her fists, she made a motion around her shoulders as though she were wrapping herself in a blanket or a cloak.

He shook his head slightly and shrugged. "I don't converse with people who refuse to use their voice."

Aizel's head snapped back at his callous tone. Although she hadn't actually expected any kindness from a Quotidian soldier, she couldn't help the tears that immediately flooded her eyes.

She turned away from him, holding her shoulders high as she all but stomped to her horse.

A soldier stepped forward to help her mount the horse, but she ignored him. Using the half wall, she mounted the animal herself, keeping her face turned away from the prince as they trotted out of the courtyard.

Perhaps it was better he was cruel and mean. It would make it that much easier to carry out her task.

CHAPTER 16

$\mathcal{E}$rich hunched over his horse as he gently urged it forward with his knees.

He felt . . . guilty.

He had seen the tears in the girl's eyes before she'd turned away from him. He had never made someone cry before. Not even his sister. Sure, he had teased Meena until she got angry and yelled back at him, but he had never, ever made her cry.

He had not intended to be cruel . . . It was just . . . every time the Majis girl looked at him, her eyes were shadowed and angry. Her demeanor was obvious; she was cold.

Her motives, however, were less obvious. Why hadn't she just asked for a cloak? Was she trying to appear helpless and small to garner his sympathy? If so, she was absolutely succeeding.

The tears in her eyes, though, were a surprise. She had looked genuinely rejected.

He was surprised that she had feelings, which made him

feel quite silly. How could someone who had destroyed dozens of lives at once still have feelings?

"You killed my men," he should have said. *"You think I care about your minor comfort when you destroyed innocent lives?"* He had been right to ignore her request.

While he tried to exonerate himself from guilt, they left the tall, protective walls of the monastery, and the morning breeze hit his face. It was a chilly morning, and he was wearing multiple layers of wool and leather.

He wanted to turn around and see if she felt the cold, too. His mind could not unsee the image of her standing in front of him, hugging her arms around her small frame . . . her big green eyes gazing up at him, begging him to understand her wordless plea.

And her hair. Her fiery hair cascaded in windswept waves around her shoulders, reflecting the sunlight in the most intense shade of bright red he had ever seen. He thought it was brown. Had it changed color?

He shook himself, opening his eyes to the real world around him. He'd seen her in a dark room when her hair was wet. She looked different in the sunlight. That was all.

And that was exactly what she wanted him to think—that she was weak, innocent. She was trying to get him to let down his guard.

He wouldn't fall for it. He wouldn't let the sorceress work her magic on him.

They had barely traveled a league from the monastery when frantic hoofbeats pounded behind them.

"Councilor Turio!" a bellowing voice called.

Erich pulled his horse to a stop and turned to see Mingus riding toward them.

"Councilor Turio," he called again. "We received urgent

news this morning from Chendas. General Gautho needs you back at the monastery immediately."

At that, the councilor turned his horse to face the messenger. "Did he say what is so urgent?"

"No." Mingus shook his head. "Just that you must return."

"Very well." The councilor sighed. His wrinkled skin looked rather flushed in the brisk morning air.

Erich squeezed his knees lightly, and his horse moved back in the direction of the monastery.

Mingus shook his head, holding out a hand. "No, not her." He paused, breathing heavily. "The general don't want her back under his responsibility. Continue your journey to Chendas."

Confused, Erich cut his eyes at the councilor. He hadn't feared the girl yesterday, but after her manipulative tactic this morning, he was no longer quite so naïve. "She's too dangerous to return to a building full of warriors, but not so dangerous that I can't escort her across two kingdoms alone?" Something felt off about this.

The councilor urged his horse forward until he was by Erich's side. "She is harmless without her voice, Your Highness." His whisper was barely audible. "She could turn the tide of this war. The general himself said it: you are the best he has got. You can do this."

Erich felt the weight of responsibility settle onto his shoulders, and he sat taller on his horse. "She cannot speak?"

The councilor raised his eyebrows—or what would have been his eyebrows if there were any hair left above his eyes. "Whatever you do," he whispered, "do not remove the ribbon." He tapped his own neck lightly.

Erich's eyes darted back to the girl.

The tip of her nose was quite pink.

Erich pushed the thought away. Why had he even noticed that?

She was indeed wearing a white ribbon around her neck. A dark rock hung from its center.

Why hadn't he noticed it before? Perhaps the bright green of her eyes had distracted him from looking anywhere else.

Blinking rapidly, he turned his attention back to the councilor, relief flooding through him. She couldn't use her magic without her voice.

Turio was also staring at the girl. There was an odd smirk behind his thinning beard that disappeared quickly as Erich noticed it. When the councilor turned back to him, his expression was completely serious. "You can do this. I'll catch up with you if I can or send a messenger after you."

Erich gave a single nod, and the old man quickly rode back toward the waiting Mingus.

He could do this. He would ignore her flaming red hair and pleading eyes and carry this task out for the safety of his kingdom and his people.

CHAPTER 17

The prince spent the entire day riding just behind
Aizel.

Every time she turned to look at him, his eyes were glued
to her in concentration.

She felt uncomfortable with the way he stared at her, as
though he was afraid she would escape if he so much as
blinked.

Alarmed at the thought, she glanced at him once again
from the corner of her eye. He was still staring at her, and it
was a full seven seconds before he finally did blink.

At least he was blinking. Somehow, that made him less
scary.

He never said a word to her. Eventually, Aizel forgot
about his angry eyes as she lost herself in the beauty of the
landscape around her. She had never left her small island
home, and the tall trees and towering mountains in the
distance were more beautiful than she had ever imagined.

The area immediately surrounding them was more

familiar—softly rolling hills that were covered with sandy grass. As silverreign was melting into greenreign, colorful flowers blossomed everywhere she looked.

Aizel marveled at the soft pastel shades of the delicate petals. They were so much softer than the vibrant hues on Istroya. She wanted to slide off her horse and run up the nearest hill, scooping up every shade of flower she saw.

As the sun fell, the prince slowed down, sauntering off the road for a little way before coming back.

"I'm looking for a good spot to camp," he said, speaking to her for the first time since that morning.

She nodded in understanding. *Obviously*, she thought. *I've only been doing this exact thing for days on end.*

"This northern route has few towns," he continued, his voice light. But as soon as he'd finished speaking, he turned away from her quickly as though remembering who she was. "Don't expect comfortable accommodations." His final words were gruff.

Aizel nodded again, even though he was no longer looking at her.

A few moments later, he slid from his mount. Grabbing the reins of her horse in one hand and his in the other, he veered them off the narrow main road into a shallow valley.

A small copse of trees huddled around a flowing stream that cut through the basin of the valley. Dense, overgrown meadows filled the rest of the area, spreading over the gentle hills back toward the main road.

The prince led the horses straight to the stream so they could drink. As her spotted horse dipped her head down, the mare's body tilted forward at an uncomfortable angle. Alarmed, Aizel gripped its mane and jumped off the tall animal.

Her bare feet landed hard on the rocky riverbank, and small shivers of pain shot up through her ankles. She quickly restabilized, reminding herself not to dismount so quickly next time.

The prince ignored her.

She patted her horse in an awkward attempt at an apology—since she had grabbed her poor mane so tightly— and wandered back toward the copse of trees.

The ground was covered in a thick layer of deep-green grass that appeared to have small, circular leaves. Airy purple flowers grew atop the green bedding. The flowers were perfectly spherical, and Aizel wanted to know what it would feel like to hold an entire handful of them.

Unable to restrain herself, she dropped down, hunching over the balls of her feet so she could pick a small bouquet.

"You will not stray out of my sight." The prince's harsh voice sounded immediately behind her, and she jumped forward with a voiceless yelp.

Turning to face him, she held out her cupped hands full of flowers, hoping to show him she was doing the most harmless thing she could imagine.

He jumped backward at the gesture. She rolled her eyes at his skittish behavior.

A small part of her mind wanted to find out how far she could push his comfort. Readjusting her hands, she picked one of the flowers and held it out to him, opening her eyes wide.

He looked from the flower to her face, clearly confused, but made no move to accept her offering.

Shrugging, she gave him a small smile and dropped back to the ground to continue gathering a fuller bouquet.

By the time the sun fully set, he had built a small fire in

the center of the glade. She sat down opposite him, basking in the warmth of the flames.

She arranged the spherical flowers into a small mountain in front of her legs, enjoying the way they rolled off but also seemed to cling to each other. Choosing three, she slipped them into the small sack at her side.

As she reached inside the bag, her hand touched the vial. Her spine froze as her stomach tightened. For a moment, she'd forgotten she was carrying poison.

She glanced at the prince, almost afraid he could read her thoughts. He was removing food from his saddlebags.

Watching him, she considered what it would take to get a few drops of her poison onto the food he was about to eat.

The thought made her stomach turn, and she quickly pulled her hand from the bag. She had multiple days to carry out her assignment; she didn't need to worry about it quite yet. It would be better for him to take her most of the way to her destination first.

By the time she looked up, the prince was standing over her. She started, guilt piercing through her.

Had he seen what was in her bag?

"Are you saving flowers?"

She stared up at him, nodding as innocently as she could.

"Why . . . never mind." He handed her a piece of dried meat and a waterskin from his saddlebags.

Her stomach rumbled as she accepted them gratefully.

He spent the evening glaring into the flames. It was such a far cry from the boy who had charmed everyone in the courtyard of that stone fort.

Feeling no pity for his self-induced attitude, Aizel yawned and glanced at the ground around her. The area surrounding their small fire was well padded with the dense leafy grass and looked far more comfortable than some of the places she had recently slept.

Checking the area for any hidden stones or sticks, she lowered herself onto her side.

At her motion, the prince finally pulled his eyes from the fire and stood. She watched from the corner of her eye as he, too, stretched and made his way over to the saddlebags. When he turned back to face her, he was carrying a blanket. Instead of returning to his side of the fire, he rounded to hers and held out the blanket.

Sitting up on her elbow, she reached up to accept it from him.

His other hand held a length of rope.

She sighed. Turio had told the soldiers there was no need to keep her from escaping, so she had remained relatively free during the second half of the last trip. Of course, he had not passed that information on to the prince. *"She will not run away because she is trying to kill you."* That would have gone over well.

Knowing it was useless, she shook her head at the prince; she had to at least try.

The prince shrugged. "I can't let you escape."

She pointed to the ribbon around her neck, indicating her lack of voice and lack of power.

"How do I know you won't take it off?" he countered.

She shook her head.

"Like I'm going to believe you. I can't even take your word for it since you can't even speak."

Was he laughing at her? She scowled up at him, pointing rapidly to herself and shaking her head. *"I can't remove it."* The words she could not say out loud burned in her throat, as though the ribbon itself was holding them back.

"You won't remove it, or you can't remove it?" He seemed to be speaking to himself, as if he had just realized the difference.

Aizel nodded emphatically. Was that why he had been watching her so closely all day? This Quotidian prince did not even know how a muting necklace worked!

"That doesn't mean you won't get up and stab me in the back," he said. "I'm not an idiot, Azel. That takes no magic."

It was the second time he had said her name, and he was still pronouncing it wrong. She sighed dramatically and held out her hands, wrists together.

He stepped closer and tied the rope around her wrists, attaching the other end around a nearby tree and leaving her quite a bit of room to move around. At least she was still close to the warmth of the fire.

When he had returned to his own spot, she took the blanket and awkwardly spread it around herself despite her bound hands. The last thing she saw as she drifted off to sleep was the distant expression of his eyes, staring once again into the flames across the fire.

The sound of a log hitting the fire woke her with a start.

The prince was still awake, and the fire lapped hungrily at its new fuel.

The arm she was lying on felt as though it were being stabbed by hundreds of needles, so she had been asleep for some time. She adjusted her position, wondering why the prince wasn't trying to sleep himself. Was he keeping guard, afraid of some outside attack? Or was he still afraid of her despite the fact she couldn't reach him?

Regardless of the answer, it wasn't her problem to solve. Lying back down in a more comfortable position, she closed her eyes and drifted back to sleep.

The sound of a scream broke into her dreams. She sat up quickly, wide awake.

The sky was still completely dark, but the fire had burned down to a pile of hot coals.

She glanced around the small area, looking for the source of the scream.

The prince muttered something she couldn't hear, and she looked across at him. He was lying on his back with his face toward her. In the dim light of the embers, she could see his eyes were closed.

Muttering something else, he lifted his hands and started pushing air away from his face.

"*Wake up!*" Aizel instinctively shouted, but the words caught in her throat. "*You're dreaming!*"

His hands continued to move, waving dangerously close to the burning hot coals.

Aizel jumped up, moving around the fire to shake him awake, but her bound hands stopped her. He hadn't left her enough slack to reach him.

She watched him for another moment, yanking on the rope in the vain hope it might break. Nothing happened.

He groaned in his sleep. Whatever nightmare he was having sounded horrible. His arms waved more frantically, swinging directly over the glowing embers.

Pulling herself as far as she could, Aizel lifted her foot and swung it out toward him. Her heel landed hard against his shoulder.

He jolted awake.

The swinging motion had thrown her off balance, and she felt her body tumbling toward the hot coals. She yanked on the rope, propelling herself toward the tree and over the dying fire. She landed painfully on her shoulder, but she was otherwise fine.

Her heart beating quickly, she sat back up and turned to face the prince.

He was sitting up fully now and breathing heavily. His face appeared damp, reflecting the reddish light of the embers he had barely escaped.

"I was having the nightmare again." It wasn't a question.

She nodded.

His breathing was ragged, but he forced a smile on his face. "Sorry to wake you. It wasn't really that bad."

Clearly it was, or you wouldn't have been screaming, Aizel responded in her head. Lifting her hands, she opened her palms as much as she could in a questioning gesture. *"What were you dreaming?"*

He shook his head. "I hardly remember," he answered as though he had easily understood what she'd tried to communicate. "Go back to sleep." He lay back down, turning his back to her.

"You're welcome for waking you out of it," she whispered wordlessly at him as she pulled her blanket back around her.

"Thank you for waking me." His words were so quiet, Aizel wasn't sure she had even heard them.

But a small smile flickered across her face as she once again closed her eyes to sleep. For the first time in a month, she'd almost had a real conversation with someone.

CHAPTER 18

The following morning, Erich woke with the sun. He didn't enjoy sleeping on the hard ground, but he had definitely grown used to it.

His first thought, of course, was the girl in his charge.

She was still asleep, curled into a ball with her knees tucked under her chin. She looked so innocent—vulnerable even.

Erich turned away, ashamed. He felt like a monster for dragging a girl who could have been his younger sister through the open woods and tying her to a tree.

What would the Council do with her? He shook that thought from his mind and went to bathe his face in the crisp, fresh water of the stream. That wasn't his problem. She deserved the justice she would get. She was not innocent. She was a Majis—a cruel, bloodthirsty magic-wielder—and he would do well not to forget that fact.

The cold water washed the last bit of sleep from his eyes.

Returning to the campsite, he slipped his arms into the

gray jacket of his uniform, ignoring the weight of it as the leather armor settled onto his shoulders.

He could not let his guard down, and wearing the stiff, gray outfit would help him remember he was always on duty.

Behind him, he could hear the Majis girl sit up. She kept the blanket wrapped around her shoulders as she yawned herself into wakefulness.

Erich ignored her and went to his saddlebag to dig out some food.

A deep thump sounded behind him, and he whipped around.

The girl was back on the ground, lying on her side, her face grimacing in pain.

Avoiding his gaze, she pushed herself back into a sitting position and reached down for her foot. Handling it with great care, she lightly ran her fingers over a large, puffy red bruise that covered her entire ankle.

Erich had seen a similar injury when Onric had fallen from a tall window as a boy. It had been a horrible accident, and Onric had cried for days while he was unable to walk.

The girl's eyebrows pinched together as she used her good foot to push herself back onto her feet.

Erich jumped forward instinctively, knowing what would happen the second she put weight on her bad foot.

Sure enough, as she gingerly shifted her weight, her leg gave out. She collapsed onto the ground, her face twisted in a soundless scream.

Erich reached her too late to catch her, but he knelt at her side and quickly undid the rope around her wrists. "How did that happen?" he asked, unable to miss the single tear running down her cheek and the pained way her upper teeth were biting into her lower lip.

After rubbing her wrists, she tilted her face onto her free hands and closed her eyes, pretending to be asleep.

The motion confused him at first, until he realized she was answering his question with her hands instead of her mouth. He watched her intently.

She lifted her head and used her good foot to mimic kicking him.

"When you kicked me awake last night?" he asked.

She nodded.

"That must have been quite some kick," he said, rubbing his shoulder. He wasn't in pain from it. He narrowed his eyes at her. Was this some sort of trick?

She shook her head, her lips pursed.

"That's not what happened?" he asked, confused and slightly relieved.

She nodded and made to stand again.

Erich held out his hands to steady her.

Once on her good foot, she held her wrists together and reached them toward the tree over his shoulder, then made a move as though she were kicking him around the fire. Then she wobbled in his arms and sank in a controlled motion back to the ground.

Erich looked down at her, trying to decipher her movements. "You lost your balance when you kicked me because you couldn't reach around the fire."

She nodded vigorously.

"Serves you right for kicking me awake," Erich muttered, unable to pass up the opportunity for a good jest.

She didn't seem to appreciate it. She spun around on the ground so her back was facing him and hugged her knees.

Erich dropped to one knee behind her. "I didn't mean that. I was jesting." He paused. He owed her nothing. But she had hurt herself attempting to help him. He could see from the color of the bruise that she was truly in pain. "I am grateful you woke me up. Let me look at your foot."

She didn't move.

Erich waited for a few moments, then stood and grabbed another chunk of dried meat from his pack. He circled around her and held out the food.

She reached up and accepted it, nibbling it as she huddled in place.

"Let me take a look at your foot," Erich repeated. "Just to make sure no bones are broken."

She slowly lifted her knee and stretched out her leg in front of her so that the hurt foot was visible.

Taking that as a yes, Erich dropped to his knees and reached out. He touched her foot gently, avoiding the injury itself.

The entire area around the bruise was hot to the touch, but from what he could see, no cuts or scrapes had opened the skin.

Slowly moving his hands down, he ran his fingers over the swollen area as gently as he could.

A slight intake of breath brought his eyes back up to her face.

She had frozen in place, watching his every move as though she were a scared cornered animal.

Erich returned his eyes to her foot.

She seemed afraid he would hurt her.

The thought was unnerving and almost funny. He was the one who should be afraid of her, not the other way around.

And he was afraid of her. He had seen the results of her doing, even if he hadn't seen her perform the act itself.

He wondered what she would look like while using

magic. Would she still seem so young and innocent? Or would her unusual green eyes be filled with anger and vindictiveness like the Majis he had witnessed at the ball? He had trouble imagining this small, expressive girl looking at all like the hooded sorcerer who had darkened the room around him, casting a ball of light at Ian and Aden.

Gently, he squeezed his fingers around her ankle, trying to feel whether any bones were broken.

Her leg twitched, and her breath caught again. She reached forward, pushing him away. She was shaking her head quickly, her face scrunched in pain.

"I'm just checking for broken bones," he said, looking back up at her wide, frightened eyes. "I'm not trying to hurt you."

She glared at him, blinking rapidly. The distrust in her eyes cut him to the core, making him feel like he was the monster.

Trying to ignore the guilt that washed over him, he looked back down. She was making him feel soft, weak, kind. She was pretending to be innocent. She was using her wiles on him, and he wasn't going to fall for her cheap tricks. He needed to keep his feelings in check and focus on the task assigned to him, especially if that meant keeping her in her place.

"Not that it matters if I do hurt you," he muttered, gently reaching for her ankle again. "You are a Majis. A monster. A murderer."

She slapped him across the face. It happened so quickly he hadn't even seen it coming.

Startled, he jumped out of her reach.

She glared at him through angry eyes as she carefully pulled her whole leg back to herself, cradling her hurt foot.

In turn, Erich reached up a hand to cover his stinging cheek. Her reaction had been so sudden but not unwarranted. Yet the look on her face was not domineering or even angry. It was . . . hurt.

She shook her head at him, her eyes filled with pain and reproach.

Erich didn't think he'd ever said anything so rude to another person. He jumped to his feet and turned his back to avoid her disappointed gaze. "Gah!" He threw out his hands. "This is all so confusing!" He felt like an idiot. "Of course I wouldn't hurt you—that's not what I meant. I'm not like that."

Of course, it remained quiet behind him.

He turned around to gauge her reaction. "I'm not like that," he repeated, pleading with her to believe him. "It's not my place to see what justice you face. Even my father, a king, doesn't dole out punishments or rewards on a whim. He said he used to, but then he realized his place as King is not just as some dispenser of what people deserve. That's not what I mean either. I'm overexplaining things."

Hugging her knees, the girl's wide eyes followed him as he paced across the small glade.

"What I'm trying to say," Erich continued, "is that this is very confusing and you are confusing me." He paused, raking his hand through his hair.

He knew he didn't need to explain himself, not to her, but she was sitting there actively listening and he did need to sort this out.

"I don't enjoy doing this," he said. "I've never transported prisoners before. And I am angry that I have to, but someone has to do it. I can't let you go free to bring death and destruction to my kingdom and my father's people. I have a responsibility to them. You did this to yourself. You chose to use your magic to kill dozens of my men in that shipwreck. So don't look up at me with those sad green eyes like I'm hurting you. I'm not."

Running out of things to say, Erich placed his hands on his hips and looked down at her.

Her lips were pursed. Shaking her head emphatically, she pointed at him.

"No?" he said. "No, me?"

She waved a flat palm through the air and closed her eyes. It felt as though she were dismissing what he had said.

"You don't believe me?" Erich asked. "What is there not to believe?"

She pointed to herself, still shaking her head, then pointed to him again.

"No, you?" Erich said, trying to decipher her meaning. "No, me? No to both of us."

She pointed at him very emphatically, then dropped her finger. Then, she shook her head very quickly. Finally, she pointed at herself.

"Me. No. You," Erich said slowly. "I. No. You . . . I don't know you."

She nodded, her face lightening briefly.

"Of course, I don't know you," Erich said. "But I know what you are, and that's all I need to know."

She shook her head again, her face taking on an almost wild expression. She repeated her earlier motion. Pointing at him, shaking her head, and then pointing at herself.

"I do know what you are," Erich repeated. He felt as misunderstood as she seemed to. "You are a powerful monster who doesn't care about the harm and suffering you bring to others."

Her forehead wrinkled again as her expression fell. Averting her eyes, she shook her head, as though too tired to fight her point.

Erich crossed his arms, even more confused. She didn't seem proud of her evil accomplishments. Her expression held sorrow at his accusations, not glee.

As frustrating as this one-sided conversation was, Erich didn't like leaving things misunderstood. "You're still shaking your head. I'm wrong about you."

Lifting her eyes to his once more, she dropped her head for a single nod.

In that moment, Erich believed her. Her expression was so sincere.

He turned away quickly, cupping his hands around his eyes to block his vision. "Of course you are acting sincere. You are trying to sway me in your favor, exactly as Councilor Turio said you would."

He stalked toward his horse, keeping his back to her. He couldn't bear to look back at those big, sad, green eyes.

CHAPTER 19

*A*izel hugged her knees. The Quotidian hated the Majis. She had accepted that fact her entire life. This was different. She was beginning to feel as invisible and worthless as these people seemed to see her. The indifference was more painful than the hatred.

She wasn't a murderer. Clearly, Turio or the king had fed the prince some sort of lie about what had happened that day. And she had no way to tell him she'd had nothing to do with the killing of his men. Did he truly believe her magic was powerful enough to cause such a massive wave?

And he kept acting as though her magic were evil. His people had magic, and it was much, much worse.

"I'm not a monster!" she wanted to yell at his back. *"Stop calling me that."*

But you are a monster. The small thought crept into her aching mind. *Or you will be when you kill this confused stranger. You are about to become a murderer. You will be everything he has accused you of.*

"Go away!" she yelled at the voice inside her head. Her lips moved, but no sound came out.

Burying her face in her knees, she wished she could hide from view.

"It's time to get going," the prince called from where he stood by the horses. The tone of his voice was distant, as though they hadn't just had a heated conversation.

Slowly lifting her head, Aizel repositioned her body so she could stand on her good foot. She felt more exhausted this morning than she had last night.

Before she stood, she repositioned the blanket around her shoulders so she wouldn't have to stoop and grab it off the ground.

With tremendous care, she pushed herself up and balanced on one leg.

She wobbled slightly and instinctively set her bad foot on the ground. Just that slightest motion shot thousands of needles of pain up her foot all the way to her knee.

She exhaled through gritted teeth.

The foot she had twisted was not the one she'd kicked the prince with last night; it was the one she'd been standing on when she'd stumbled backward. It had been mildly painful then, but she'd fallen asleep assuming it would be fine in the morning.

Now she stood helplessly in the center of the glade, staring at the horses, which were at least some seven steps away.

She didn't want to show weakness in front of the man who had just insulted her. She couldn't. But if she attempted to take a single step forward, she would crumple to the ground again, and that would be a far worse blow to her pride.

"Never ask for help. Especially from a Quotidian," she whispered to herself soundlessly.

So, she stood where she was, biting her lower lip as she scrambled to think of any other option. Maybe she could manage it if she crawled?

The prince still stood with his back to her. "Coming?" His voice was curt.

"*No!*" she yelled at his back. *"I can't move, idiot."*

Finally, he turned back toward her. His eyebrows were stretched high, and a sigh of exasperation escaped his lips. He looked as though he were about to say something, but then he shut his mouth. "Oh, right," he finally muttered.

Aizel crossed her arms and pinched her nose in an effort not to cry. She hated feeling helpless.

He crossed the glade back to her. "I'm going to . . . Can I pick you up?"

Avoiding eye contact, she nodded. The thing she most wanted was to be as far away from him as possible, which was the complete opposite of allowing him to put his arms around her.

Bending down, he swung one arm under her knees and the other under her lower back.

She grabbed his neck so she could support some of her own weight and kept her body as stiff as possible.

In a few short moments, he had lifted her onto her horse. He stood close while she settled herself gratefully on the familiar animal.

She lifted the bundled blanket from her shoulders and held it down to him. He watched her closely, but his expression had returned to a stony iciness.

"Keep it," he said, pushing it back toward her. "Today might still be chilly."

CHAPTER 20

By the time they stopped for the night, Aizel's ankle throbbed painfully. She had protected it as best she could, but the constant motion of the horse had slowly taken its toll.

She looked down at the ground beneath her, contemplating jumping down by herself and trying to land on her good foot. The thought of even slightly jostling her aching ankle kept her in place.

Erich slid from his mount, letting the animal wander to the nearby stream by herself.

Seeing where its companion was headed, Aizel's mount stepped forward to follow. Erich caught her reins. "Not quite yet, Constance."

Aizel patted her horse's neck, unaware that she had a name. Aizel mouthed the foreign word, rolling her tongue in an attempt to make the new sounds despite her silent breathing.

"I don't know if that's her name," Erich said. He must

have noticed her action. "I just took to calling her that since she is so steady."

Aizel nodded in understanding. She wanted to smile. A horse with a name was more endearing than a horse without one.

"Ready to dismount?" Erich reached his hands up toward her.

Aizel nodded. Having no other option, she released her hold on Constance's reins and slid down toward Erich.

Instead of catching her under her armpits as she expected, he scooped her off the animal with one arm under her knees and the other under her shoulders as he had that morning.

"This way is safest for your foot."

He must have noticed her muscles tensing at his touch.

"Log or grass?" he asked, indicating the available areas for her to sit.

Not wanting to be perched on top of anything else, Aizel removed one hand from his shoulder and pointed to the ground.

"Grass it is." He gently lowered her to a soft patch of the same fluffy grass she had slept on the previous night.

Aizel stretched out on the firm ground, rearranging the blanket she still had on her shoulders. The grass tickled her sensitive, swollen ankle, but it felt cooling at the same time.

She picked a single strand of the strange grass, twirling it in her fingers and watching the three round leaves flutter through the air. If only she had something to press it with, she could preserve the pretty leaves to show Celesta.

She slipped it into her sack regardless. Sometimes things dried more interestingly than she expected, and the little piece of grass made her happy.

Erich approached her a few moments later. He was wringing the excess water out of a length of sopping wet cloth. "This might help." He dropped to one knee and lightly wrapped it around her lower leg.

It did help. The cold water instantly soothed the burning ache.

Aizel was confused. He kept calling her horrible things, but his actions were—for the most part—thoughtful and even a little kind.

"Why are you helping me?" she wanted to ask. *"You clearly hate me."*

Speaking to Celesta with her hands was so familiar that Aizel was already imagining how she could ask those same questions without her voice.

Slumping her shoulders, she held back. If it were Celesta, the conversation would have been seamless. Her sister was so easy to talk to. But Aizel was now realizing how vulnerable it made her feel to speak with her hands and her actions. Doing so required asking for the full attention of the listener.

To be vulnerable with this prince was to put herself at his mercy. And she was already at his mercy in every other way.

After they ate another meal of the same dried meat that everyone on this continent seemed to live on, Aizel gratefully relaxed onto her side. There was no comfortable way to sit on the ground with her hurting foot.

She missed the familiar food of Istroya. It might be scarce, but it was always fresh—especially the fish and the fruit.

Getting up from the fire, the prince reached into his bag and pulled out the length of rope. As he rounded the fire toward her, she leaned away, shaking her head.

His eyebrows drew together over his heartless eyes.

She pointed to her ankle. Certainly, he didn't think she was going to get up and run away when she was so badly injured.

"It's still too risky."

She rolled her eyes. As he reached down toward her, she grabbed his wrist and placed it over her own.

He looked at her with no comprehension on his face. This boy was an idiot.

She grabbed the rope from his hand and wrapped it around their wrists.

"You want me to tie our wrists together for the night?"

She nodded.

"What difference does that make?"

She pointed to her foot, then back at him.

He didn't understand.

She placed her head in her hand to indicate sleeping, then she shook her head with her eyes still closed to indicate having a nightmare. Then, she pointed from him to her ankle.

It's your fault this happened to me. The words were burning in her throat, but she couldn't release them.

"You got hurt last night because you couldn't reach me and you couldn't speak to me," he said as realization seemed to dawn on him.

She nodded. Finally.

"Just because you can't do magic without your voice doesn't mean I trust you," he said. "I don't trust you at all. For all I know, this is just some sort of a giant manipulative scheme by an evil sorceress. But I will tie your hand to mine tonight since you cannot get away. If you try anything at all —even just an attempt to untie the knots—I will feel it immediately and wake up."

She did not deign to respond to his monologue with a nod. His use of the words "evil" and "manipulative" made her feel small. She knew he was basing his insults on the lies he'd heard, but they still hurt.

Not wanting to be stuck to a tree, helpless, without motion or voice, she nevertheless held out her hand and allowed him to tie a snug knot around her wrist.

He then attached the rope to his wrist, leaving an arm's length of room between them.

That night, she had trouble falling asleep, worried as she was that any motion of her hand would wake and anger him.

She could tell that he was awake, too. Though his hand remained motionless, his breathing was shallow and uneven, and he frequently repositioned his head.

Eventually, her mind gave in to her exhausted body, and she drifted off.

She was awoken by a sharp tug from the rope on her hand and small, strangled yells coming from the prince.

"No, no," he said in his sleep. "You're not listening to me. I said we shouldn't do it. They attack from the sea."

Aizel leaned up on her elbow and grasped the rope in her hand, pulling it toward herself.

"No!" he screamed. "I'm caught in the rigging, let me go. I can't breathe!"

Aizel immediately stopped pulling the rope. She was intensifying the nightmare of his drowning experience rather than waking him from it.

Using her elbows, she pulled herself across the ground to get closer to him, wincing in pain as her foot dragged on the grass behind her.

Reaching out, she shook his shoulder. *"Wake up, you're only dreaming."* She shook him again.

He sat up before he was even fully awake, panting heavily. Reaching down toward his hand, he tore at the knotted rope.

Aizel reached forward, pulling at the loop to help him remove it after his first few attempts failed.

He tossed the rope out of reach as soon as he was free. He was breathing heavily, his face once again covered in sweat.

Aizel sat up, scooting herself back to her blanket as he calmed himself.

Avoiding her gaze, he grabbed a large stick and poked the coals of the dying fire back to life.

Aizel leaned into the welcome heat, watching him carefully from the side of her vision. She made a loop of continuous circles in the air with her finger. *Do you have these nightmares every night?"*

The motion finally forced him to look at her, and he stared at her for a moment as though not comprehending.

Aizel dropped her hand. He didn't deserve her sympathy.

He looked back at the fire for a few moments. "Is this a recurring problem?" he finally asked, vocalizing her question.

She looked back at him and nodded.

"More recently, yes." He kept his eyes on the flames. "Sorry I woke you. I'm not very tired anymore. You can go back to sleep."

Aizel shrugged. After waking to his scream, she wasn't very tired anymore either.

CHAPTER 21

*E*rich wanted to put out the fire so he could be alone in the dark. The dream had conjured up all the horrible emotions he had felt during the shipwreck. His body felt just as taut and on edge as it had been then.

And she had witnessed it all. He had definitely been screaming in his dream, but had he screamed out loud as well?

His wrist burned, and he rubbed it with his opposite hand. He tried to tell himself he wasn't tied to a sinking mast and that everything was fine, but his body refused to believe him.

Maybe if he slowed his breathing, his heart would finally slow as well.

But the slower he breathed, the more lightheaded he felt.

He would rather stay up for the rest of the night than experience the dream again.

For some reason, she was still sitting up as well. He could see her eyes darting toward him from the side.

He dropped his shoulders. His cream undershirt was soaked through, leaving his back exposed to the cold. He didn't want to grab his gray doublet from the pack, though. He was tired of being on duty. Picking up his blanket instead, he wrapped it around himself, protecting his back from the cold as the new flames of the fire warmed him from the front.

"Azel," he said, hoping the girl across the fire would leave him in peace. "Go to sleep."

She shook her head and shrugged.

Erich held his hands out to the fire. Rather than annoy him, her wakeful presence was surprisingly welcome. Perhaps if they found something to talk about, he could distract himself.

"Do you ever have nightmares?" If he wanted her to stay awake, he couldn't make her angry.

She raised her eyebrows, then dropped her eyes to the fire and nodded.

"What are they about?"

She stared at the fire, her eyes going to a faraway place.

Erich realized too late that she had no way to answer his question. He would have to design his questions better. "Are they always about the same thing?"

Instead of answering, she looked up and pointed at him, throwing his question back over the fire.

It was Erich's turn to look away. The whole point of this was not to revisit his nightmares—but then, he had been the one to start this conversation. "I don't believe in nightmares."

Azel didn't respond.

"Not that I don't believe they exist," Erich continued, having nothing else to say. "I just don't believe in them. I don't believe in being scared of things. If you spend your whole life in fear, you are boxing yourself in." Erich felt himself warming up. This was a conversation Aden would have loved.

Aden.

He hoped his brother had not succumbed to the curse.

"Take my father, for example. He's spent his whole life preparing his kingdom for an attack. He's always lived on the defensive, but what if he'd had a chance to focus his energy on increasing methods of farming so the outer holds could acquire more wealth? Or Ian, my oldest brother. He's going to be the future king someday, and he's so afraid of breaking the rules that he's never truly relaxed and won't let himself enjoy things with Onric and me. So, no, I've never had nightmares before. And these past few weeks have been pretty terrible. But I'm really okay with it, because I'm not going to let a few hours of fear in the middle of the night hold me back. All that to say, I don't believe in nightmares. I'm not like my father or Ian, and I won't make all my decisions based on fear." Erich felt great about that revelation. He'd made up half of it as he went, but it was all true. Aden would indeed have been proud. He could talk about these things for hours on end. Feeling very proud of himself, Eric looked up at the girl across the fire.

She didn't look impressed at all.

Eric shrank back.

Her eyes were wide, staring at him with a complicated mix of disbelief and concern. Her mouth hung open, and she scrunched her nose as her eyebrows drew together.

She looked away, rubbing her chest right below the gem on her throat. Her mouth twisted into a confused smile as she slowly shook her head.

Finally, she turned back to face him, her face confident and assured. She pointed at him and mouthed the word, *"No."*

No? Everything he'd said was true. What did she know about him to deny that?

Using her face and hands, she made a few quick gestures Erich instantly understood. "I'm afraid of you?"

She nodded decisively.

"I'm not." He immediately defended himself, not stopping to think whether it was true. He was not scared of her at the moment, at least. "Besides, what does that have to do with anything?"

Her expression said he was stupid for not knowing the answer to his own question.

He pulled his hands away from the fire and braced them around his crossed knees. He didn't want to think about whether his fear of her meant anything, but now that she'd posed the question, he had to know.

He stared into the soft flames, biting his lips together between his teeth. "My fear of you is justified," he said, still feeling defensive. "You have a powerful magic that hurts and kills." Just saying the words out loud reminded Erich whom he was speaking with. He didn't care about her opinion of him, and he shouldn't even be thinking about anything she said or asked him. "You are heartless and wrong, and I am not making decisions based on fear. I'm doing what is right."

Feeling more secure in his own thoughts, he looked up again to make sure she understood.

The space across the fire was empty. She was no longer sitting and listening intently to his thoughts but had curled back up away from him on the ground. Her face was buried under her arms.

Erich inhaled with a snort. Fine. He did not need her affirmation to know he was right.

Having no desire to go back to sleep, he remained as he was—ignoring the small tightness that spread through his chest.

CHAPTER 22

*A*izel cradled her head against the hard ground. She had never met anyone so stupid. Every time he showed her the slightest hint of himself, he had to follow it up by attacking her.

It was as if that stiff, gray jacket he wore was some kind of protection for his self-image and he was too afraid to take it off and be left vulnerable and weak.

She closed her eyes. Just because she couldn't respond to his heartless words didn't mean she had to listen to them. Besides, he would only be a problem for a few more days.

Her stomach churned, and she threw that thought out of her head. She had plenty of time to worry about it on a future day.

She woke a few hours later, when the bright light of the morning sun forced its way through the trees overhead.

She reached down and gently touched her ankle. It still felt warm, and she flipped her hand over to cool it with the backside of her fingers. She tried wiggling her toes but immediately stopped. If anything, the pain was worse now than it had been. It was like her ankle was sore just from being sore.

Great.

She would be reliant on the self-centered, spoiled prince all day again.

"Good morning, Azel," a sickeningly cheerful voice sounded from behind her.

"It's EYE-zell," she replied in her head, stretching herself into wakefulness. At least him saying her name wrong was better than him calling her a sorceress, monster, or murderer.

Something smelled good. She sat up and turned around to face the crackling fire.

Rising above the prince's head, elegantly swaying by the smoky fire, was the longest single feather Aizel had ever seen. Easily longer than her arm, the weightless plume was somehow sticking straight up into the air, anchored at its base by the orange cap on the prince's head.

Below the hat, the prince sported an elaborate purple suit with orange trimmings.

He watched her reaction carefully, looking very pleased with himself. For someone who had gotten very little sleep, he looked far too happy.

Her nose twitched again, distracting her with the intoxicating scent of warm food.

The prince was holding a long stick over the fire, roasting what looked like several rolls of bread. She smelled something more, though.

"I've been saving this for a good day. And today . . ." he trailed off, pausing for no apparent reason other than dramatic effect, "is a good day."

She raised her eyebrows at him. "Why?"

"It's warm, beautiful, the sun is shining. We have good food."

His list of generic reasons wasn't quite as convincing for Aizel as he'd probably hoped. *"My sister is in danger. I reek of smoke. I'm stuck with the most obnoxious person I've ever met,"* she responded in her head.

"And," Erich carried on merrily, "we might even be staying in a proper inn tonight, or tavern, if that's all they've got."

Aizel conceded that point. Sleeping indoors was a luxury she would be happy to return to.

Stepping around the fire, he handed her the cool end of the stick. "Finish roasting these, will you? I'm going to go freshen up in the stream."

She nodded, glad to have the food as close to her as possible. *"I'm not sure how much fresher you can get,"* she mentally called after him.

"Save a bite for me," he said, practically bouncing out of sight.

Aizel happily turned her attention to the roasting buns. When they looked nicely toasted, she maneuvered the long stick in her hand so that they could cool enough to touch.

A bit too impatient, she slid the first roll off the end of the stick, burning her fingers as she went.

A white, gooey substance stretched between stick and bun. There was melted cheese inside! That was what had smelled so good.

Unable to wait any longer, Aizel dove right into the roll. She had never tasted a better flavor combination than the toasted bread with tart cheese.

After finishing the first in a few mouthfuls, she reached

for the second. Her stomach mumbled its content as she licked her fingers clean.

Maybe it was a good day.

She eyed the remaining three buns. Erich had not said how many to save for him.

Suddenly, her elated feelings dissipated, and the food clogged in her throat.

This was her chance. Her heart raced, making her stomach flip.

All she had to do was reach into her bag, pull out the vial, and slip a few drops into the last bun. The flavorful cheese would likely mask the lotus flavor.

Then it would be over.

Celesta would be free.

Aizel bit her lip, glancing down at the sack on her side.

Could she do it? He didn't deserve to die. Or did he? He was living in a delusion, created by himself and others, that kept him comfortable in his own self-righteousness. He was in a position of power, a position wherein he could pass that same delusion on to so many more . . .

Aizel held the buns over the fire to keep them warm, looking for any excuse to stop the thoughts in her mind. No one deserved to die.

And she was not about to start thinking like that.

Besides, it was too early. She at least had to wait until her ankle was healed enough to carry her weight. For the moment, she needed him.

That thought calmed her, and she shoved the residual guilt from her mind.

Maybe if she saved him all three of the remaining buns, she would feel less bad about her momentary plan to assassinate him.

She had lost her appetite anyway.

"I did some thinking last night about what you said," Erich's voice sounded before he came into view. "Err, communicated." He stepped back into the clearing, hat in hand. His fingers carefully brushed out the long feather, aligning each of its vanes and barbules to achieve fluttery perfection.

She watched his hands, keeping her face as normal as possible.

"And, if I haven't been living up to my core philosophy, I've decided to change that. Starting now." He placed the hat on his head and bowed elegantly toward her.

The feather floated through the air, dipping dangerously low over the firepit and its greedy flames.

Aizel waved her free hand, trying to get his attention or reach the feather before it was too late. *"Stop! You're a walking fire hazard!"*

He glanced up at her as he rose from the bow. The feather was still dipping down over his head, and he whisked it to safety as soon as he realized what was happening.

She wasn't entirely sure what he meant by his declaration, but this was already proving to be a much better day.

As he quickly ate the remaining food, she put out the fire and stood to leave.

He fastened the saddlebags, then came back to carry her to the horses.

She held out a hand to stop him. After last night, she had decided—helpless or not—she was doing things on her own terms.

Gesturing toward Constance, she made her intentions clear. *"Bring the horse to me."*

"That's a good idea," Erich responded. "Why didn't we think of that yesterday?"

"Probably because you were too busy telling me that my feelings don't matter." She didn't have a way to communicate that with her hands, but she satisfied herself with thinking it. If only the uncomfortable pressure at the base of her throat weren't reminding her she was voiceless.

The prince brought Constance to stand next to her, then helped her mount. Aizel settled in for a day in the saddle, feeling better than she had for some time.

CHAPTER 23

*E*rich wanted to spur his horse into a swift trot. His arms were free, and he wanted to stretch them out and embrace the world. It felt so good not to be wearing the stifling gray uniform.

Azel was safely in his charge. He had no reason to be afraid of her. She couldn't do anything until a magic-wielder removed her muting necklace. He didn't have any responsibility toward her other than to see her safely into the hands of the Council in Chendas.

Surprisingly, she had been absolutely right when she'd accused him of fearing her. He had been afraid of her, and that fear had been driving his decisions. But not anymore.

He had hated himself over the last few weeks. No one was here to judge him or tell him what to wear or how to act.

A part of him had always admired Ian, and he'd always been jealous of how easily his older brother commanded respect. But Erich also spent every day thankful he was the youngest son and not the oldest. He never wanted to be as boring and responsible as Ian.

For now, with no one watching, he was going to just be Erich. He didn't care what Azel thought of him.

It was a beautiful greenreign day, and he was done being miserable.

Even his horse pranced below him as if sensing his good mood.

Erich watched the scenery change around him, marveling at how much more beautiful each tree was when he appreciated it properly.

By the time he had gazed at three trees, they were starting to look the same. So, he turned his eyes elsewhere.

On the far horizon, a range of craggy peaks met the skyline. The mountains that separated Iseldis from Chendas were tall and imposing, like a protective wall between the two kingdoms.

It was unfortunate that they weren't on the coastline, protecting Iseldis from the fickle ocean.

Despite their edge, the mountains also had an air of majestic beauty. Erich had always loved looking at them from the window of his castle bedroom.

They were amazingly beautiful mountains. But no matter how far they traveled, the mountains looked the same in the distance.

Erich brought his eyes back to the road around him.

Being happy by himself was not fun at all.

"Azel!" he said, urging his horse forward to ride next to her. "Which do you think are more beautiful, the mountains or the sea?"

She looked over at him for a moment, likely gauging

whether he had lost his mind. After a while, she gestured behind them, mouthing the word "sea."

"The sea? I think I prefer the mountains, but then I grew up closer to them."

She nodded in understanding.

"Did you grow up by the sea? Oh, of course you did." He looked away from her as he remembered her connection to the ocean.

But they weren't by the sea. They were in the middle of dry land, and he wasn't going to live in fear.

"Have you ever been in the mountains?"

She pursed her lips, then raised a single finger. She almost looked like she was enjoying herself.

Today was definitely a good day. "Once?" he guessed. "What did you think?" Then, realizing his question was difficult to answer, he reworded it. "Did you like it?"

Her eyes drifted away, and her face fell. She shook her head.

"What didn't you like about it?" Erich asked, enjoying this game of questions and wanting her to enjoy it too. "Was it too cold . . . or did you go with the wrong company?"

She looked over at him, her face open and surprised. She nodded with the smallest smile.

Erich wanted to throw his fist above his head. He had guessed correctly again. "Well, perhaps we can change that on this trip."

He happily asked her questions throughout the rest of their ride. She seemed to enjoy the interaction and responded as animatedly as she could to his simple Yes or No questions.

As the sun fell, he kept pushing them forward. "There's a village not too far ahead," he explained. "I stayed there recently, and everyone was very kind. It was a fun place to stay for the night; I'm excited to repeat the experience."

Lamp-lit windows in the distance soon proved him correct, and they pulled their horses to a stop outside a small wooden tavern.

"This is the place." Erich slipped from his horse and approached hers to help her down. "Delicious warm food. A soft bed. A close but welcoming community. Sounds good, doesn't it?"

Her smile was proof enough that she heartily agreed.

Helping her down, he again caught her in his arms. "How's the ankle?"

She grimaced.

"I don't mind," he responded. "You're easy enough to carry."

She was surprisingly light, but it made sense. She barely reached his shoulder while standing. It wasn't her fault he was taller than most men. He liked being able to scoop her off her feet, too. Not that . . . no, he stopped that thought. He was just thankful she was small enough to carry, or traveling would have been far more complicated.

"I can take your horses, my lord," a young voice sounded at his side.

Erich smiled down at the stable girl. "Thank you. See that they get a good rub down and I'll pay you well tomorrow."

She grinned back at him and grabbed the horses' reins. "Your smile is payment enough."

Erich grinned. In a few strides, he and Azel were at the door, and she reached down to slide the handle open.

Once unlatched, he kicked it slightly with his foot and strode in.

The wood-walled room was as cozy as he had remembered. Lanterns, candles, and a blazing fireplace gave the space an orange glow. The three long tables that lined the room were filled with local farmers and hunters, winding down their day with a good meal and drink. Their weather-beaten faces were pink from heat and laughter.

These were the good citizens of Iseldis. Innocent, friendly folk who had never hurt another person and who merely wanted to live out their days in peace.

These were the people who were threatened by every-thing the sorceress represented. Maybe spending time here at one of the tables before they retired for the night would help her understand that.

Erich decided not to hope for it. The whole point of this day was to not care what Azel thought. It didn't matter if she changed her mind about anything. She had already done a bad thing, and she would be prevented from doing further damage.

But he did want her to understand.

"Your Highness!" a pleasant voice welcomed him from across the room.

"Heidi!" Erich called back, remembering the tavern-keep's name.

The middle-aged woman deftly worked her way through the busy room, wiping her hands on a large towel that hung from the belt around her waist. "Welcome back." She leaned forward in an ungraceful attempt at a curtsy. "I didn't think we would see you again so soon. And with a guest." She winked.

Erich wished the good woman kept her establishment closer to the capital of Iseldis. He would be its most frequent patron if he had easier access to it.

"And such a pretty little lady, too," Heidi continued, her eyes taking in the girl in his arms.

Erich felt his cheeks grow warm. It must have been the heat blasting from the central fireplace.

"Although she could use a fresh scrap of clothing." The tavern-keep never stopped talking. "I'd think a prince ought to be able to handle that."

Erich looked down at Azel, who looked like she wanted to both flee and laugh at the same time.

A sharp tug of embarrassment hit him as he glanced at her clothing. She had spent most of the day and night wrapped in that blanket. He'd hardly noticed the shapeless brown dress she was still wearing. It was in desperate need of a wash, but it was also in dire need of an upgrade.

Why hadn't he noticed? Because his job was to take her to Chendas, not to take care of her.

He looked back up at Heidi, an apologetic grin on his face. "Dinner for two, my good lady," he said, his unsaid words hanging in the air between them.

Heidi's eyes had returned to Azel, and her face was appalled. "Did you find . . . Is this that sorceress you were searching for?" She matched Erich's gaze for confirmation, but she seemed to already know she had guessed the truth.

Erich felt something tighten inside him.

The two small arms around his neck tightened too. Azel was afraid.

This wasn't good. Erich dropped a tiny nod to the tavern-keep. "So, that dinner for two?"

"Find a seat, Your Highness." Her voice was flat as she turned on her heel with a huff.

Erich adjusted his grip on Azel. He held her closely but didn't dare look at her face. The second table held a few empty spaces in a row. Sitting them both down, he took his hat off and set it on the bench beside him.

Azel avoided the intrigued gazes of the other patrons seated alongside the table. Erich had the urge to reach under the table and squeeze her hand for reassurance.

Heidi had never seen a Majis before. She was just shocked.

"No one else heard," he whispered, wanting Azel to feel better.

She didn't respond.

Erich looked up at their tablemates with a broad grin. He had spent a long night here a few weeks ago, chatting into the wee hours of the morning with these good people. He didn't recognize any of the faces sitting directly with them, but surely these townsfolk would make fine company.

"It's not often we get a noble lord in these parts," one of the men said, returning his smile. "You from the capital?"

"Name's Erich," he responded, intentionally leaving out the "Prince" part.

"I'm called Loke." The man spoke slowly, as though Erich had passed some sort of test and was being rewarded with that information. "Running away with a lady your parents don't approve of?" Loke continued, smirking toward Azel.

Erich merely laughed uncomfortably to avoid answering.

Azel kept her head down.

"It looks like the lady isn't too amenable to the idea herself," another man said from further down the table. He chuckled into his drink as though the joke was only for himself, but he'd said it loud enough for the whole table to hear.

Erich smiled uncomfortably. They were merely jesting. Azel had no reason to get upset about it.

He was trying to think of a way to change the topic of conversation when Heidi appeared behind him.

She dropped a heaping plate full of stew in front of Erich along with a mug of ale. "Thank you, good lady." Erich's voice came out a little louder than he intended.

"That's it, though," Heidi responded. "I don't serve her kind here."

Erich looked back over his shoulder in shock.

Heidi was glaring at the back of Azel's head.

"Her kind?" Loke plunked his drink down on the table, narrowing his eyes at Azel. "What kind is she?"

"This here's a Majis sorceress," the tavern-keep announced loudly—and proudly. "Prince Erich here is bringing her in for execution."

Mugs and spoons slammed down as her words hit home. But despite the clamor of noise, Erich didn't miss the tiny gasp from Azel when Heidi said the word "execution." Her eyes went wide as she clenched her fists below the table.

"For justice," Erich raised his voice above the sudden barrage of questions and accusations that flew down the table toward them. "I'm bringing her in for justice. King Gareth will decide her fate."

The man sitting next to Azel rose from his seat, his face full of fear.

Erich held up his hand, wanting to defuse the situation. "She can't use her magic. It's safe. You don't have to leave."

The man dropped back in his seat but slid down the bench away from her.

"I think it's pretty clear what her fate ought to be." Loke slid his mug across the rough tabletop, gesturing toward Azel. "I heard the Majis hunt everyone who shows up on their little island. Have you killed an innocent man for sport, girl?"

Azel looked up at the man, horror in her eyes.

Erich wanted to reach across the table and punch the man in his face. Of course, Azel had never done anything of the sort. It was ridiculous to think the Majis did something so insane.

"Are you planning to curse us all, sorceress, when you get your magic back?" Loke provoked her.

Azel dropped her gaze, unable to respond to the man's taunts.

"What's wrong?" Loke continued. "Is something wrong with your tongue?"

Azel's face burned red. Her shoulders slumped as though she were trying to make herself even smaller.

Loke's face broke into a grin as he realized his words had hit home. "She can't talk, can she?"

Erich shrugged in response. What was happening here?

"The sorceress can't use magic, and she can't talk!" Loke announced, slamming his mug against the table again.

The titters of fear around the table gradually calmed down at this announcement.

Erich exhaled. Perhaps it was a good thing. If these people had nothing to fear, they would go back to their food and conversations.

Erich pushed his own plate of food toward Azel. He wouldn't let her starve because the tavern-keep was rude.

She pushed it back toward him, wrapping her arms around her stomach.

It doesn't matter, Erich told himself. *It doesn't matter what she feels.*

"Her hair is the color of blood," a loud voice said from

further down the table. "I've never seen that color before. I wonder how it got to be that way?"

"I can make a few guesses," another voice responded. Ideas flew around the room, each one more disturbing than the last.

Even though she was sitting right in the middle of the room and could hear every word they said, these people didn't seem to care. Erich sat in disbelief as he tried to drown out the horrible things he was hearing. And they weren't even about him.

He glanced toward Azel. She was clutching her fisted hands to her chest, and her body shook as she inhaled.

"It doesn't matter," Erich told himself repeatedly. "For all I know, they might be right."

"Curses," he muttered under his breath. Every single thing they were saying was completely wrong. He couldn't imagine Azel doing anything a fraction as evil as they were suggesting. He couldn't sit here and listen to this.

"Let's get out of here," he whispered, standing up and stepping behind her.

As she swung herself over the bench, he placed a hand against her back. He realized it had far more to do with protecting her than protecting the quotidian folk around him. Interesting. When had that changed?

"I'm afraid we've disrupted your good establishment, Heidi," Erich called out as he scooped Azel up from the bench. "We'll be taking our leave before we impose upon your kindness further."

Before Erich turned away from the table, Loke caught his eye. He raised his mug in a toast, a slimy grin spreading over his calloused lips.

Erich turned away and walked toward the door as

quickly as he could, kicking it open in his hurry to escape the muggy room.

Every other time he had lifted Azel, she had held herself as stiffly as possible. But tonight, her face was buried against his chest and her arms clung to his neck.

He held her gently as he headed toward the stable. He could feel her heart pounding against his chest, and he realized his own heartbeat matched hers.

"I'm sorry," he whispered to the top of her head. "I'm so sorry."

Her whole body trembled. Was she still afraid?

"We'll get far away from here tonight. So far that no one can follow us. No one will hurt you."

She clung to him in response.

He entered the stable and quickly located Constance. The stable girl joined him and resaddled both horses.

Standing by Constance's side, he made to lift Azel on top of the horse. Her small hands gripped his collar for a moment longer than usual before she let go and settled herself into the saddle.

Clutched in her hands was his favorite hat. He had forgotten it on the bench. She must have grabbed it as they were leaving.

Erich kept his hands on her waist for an extra moment. "Would you like to ride with me tonight? It's going to be dark and . . ." He could think of no other excuse, except that she looked distraught enough to tumble off the tall horse if left on her own.

She looked down at him, her green eyes full of fear and distrust. She glanced back toward the inn before nodding her assent.

A few moments later, they were both mounted on his horse, with Constance connected behind.

He wrapped his arm around her waist, stabilizing her back against his chest, and urged his horse forward into the night.

Azel's tense muscles didn't relax until they had escaped into the darkness.

CHAPTER 24

As they raced away from the horrid village, Aizel felt a deep exhaustion seep into all of her being. It was more than just her body being tired; it was a weariness she knew sleep wouldn't fix.

Behind her, she could feel Erich's heart pounding in his chest. The beat was fast and constant, and it stirred a melody deep inside her.

The horses' hooves sounded in a desperate pattern as well, echoing against the hollow road beneath their feet.

The melody in her head moved through her, getting caught and twisted between the two conflicting beats.

She wanted to reach for the songs that had always calmed her, but the unmatched rhythms of Erich's heart and the horses' hooves kept cutting the notes short in her head.

Her own breathing grew uneven as her attempts to calm failed. They were riding to safety, but her body still screamed she was in danger.

Even the horses seemed to sense her panic.

A new song, one she had never heard or sang, began to form inside her. Instead of dissipating in the discordant beats around her, this new song grew out of the chaos.

It built inside her, feeding off her fear and embarrassment and anger, filling every bit of emptiness.

Her breathing deepened and intensified. She had control over this song.

However, without a voice, she had no way to release it. As the song grew, the pressure built inside her until she was afraid she'd burst.

The feeling of control slipped through her fingers. The only sound she could hear was the pounding of the blood in her ears.

She hated them. She hated their insecurities and cruelty. She wanted to fly from the horse and run back to the village, screaming the songs she had heard the Quotidian sing. Shriek at them until they felt the pain they had inflicted upon her. If she'd had her voice, nothing could have stopped her. She hated them all.

Erich repositioned the arm he held around her stomach.

The movement brought her attention back to the moment.

His grip was firm and gentle. His head hovered over hers as he leaned forward, cradling her with his body as well as he could.

She placed her arm over his, grasping his wrist for stability.

Maybe she did not hate all of them.

She was thankful for the Quotidian prince keeping her steady on this horse while they rode away from the most terrifying situation she had ever experienced. She didn't necessarily feel positively toward him, but his thoughtful actions consistently defied his callous words.

He annoyed her, but he never made her feel the way those men and women in the tavern had. He never made her feel unsafe.

The stress of the last weeks came crashing down on her all at once. Safe. She wanted to be safe. She wanted to run off into the night and disappear.

Tears formed in her eyes, and she was too tired to blink them away.

She awoke the next morning wrapped tightly in her blanket. Her arms were free, and Erich was still sleeping, wrapped in a blanket of his own a short distance away.

If he'd had another nightmare, he hadn't woken her.

She had no memory of getting off his horse the previous night, but it felt like they had ridden in the darkness for hours.

The trees around her had changed. They were taller, darker. The ground was rockier, covered with moss of varying colors rather than grass. They must have gotten far closer to the mountains, though she couldn't see them through the trees.

There was no sign of a fire. Erich must have been just as exhausted.

Aizel sat up, hugging the blanket around her. The small motion jarred her ankle. She wouldn't be walking today. Her throat felt tight, as though still clinging to the painful words of her unsung song.

Looking at her immediate surroundings, she grabbed at the fallen sticks and leaves to at least start a pile of kindling for a morning fire.

As she disturbed the ground cover, something sparkled

beneath it. She pushed away the dirt. The rocks underneath the plants glittered like gemstones.

The rocks were as dark as coal, but their rough edges were formed by countless facets. When she moved her head, they reflected back at her in brilliant purples, blues, pinks, and even the occasional ruby red.

She pulled the nearest piece she could find from the ground and gently wiped the dirt away from it, watching the beautiful colors dance across it.

The rock reminded her of something she would have seen on the bottom of the ocean. It was beautiful.

"Carborundum." Erich's voice startled her.

Confused, she looked up at him.

"I see you've found some carborundum," he clarified, pointing to the rock in her hand.

"Carborundum." She formed the strange word with her lips. If it were just a rock, such a clunky name would be perfect. But the colorful reflections gave it an ethereal quality that "carborundum" just didn't capture. She would come up with a better name later.

She dropped the rock into her bag, adding it to her collection.

Erich was sitting up, wrapped in his blanket. "I would love to suggest we remain here for the day and just rest. I think we both could use it."

Aizel tilted her head. That sounded wonderful, but she wasn't sure she could fully relax until they were further away from that village.

"But it might be smarter to put a little more distance between ourselves and . . . last night." Erich faltered over the last words, watching her closely.

She nodded in agreement, relieved that they were thinking the same thing.

"Thank you for saving my hat, though," Erich continued, pushing himself up off the ground. The cheer in his voice felt forced, but his smile was genuine.

Aizel smiled and brushed the air with her hand. "Don't even mention it." She appreciated his lighthearted attitude and responded in kind.

"Azel." His face held concern, and she guessed it wasn't for the blanket he was folding. "Forget the things they said. They were malicious lies."

His deep brown eyes caught her gaze for a brief moment. They were filled with empathy.

Aizel exhaled as the pressure in her chest finally eased.

CHAPTER 25

"We do have one small problem," Erich said as he brought Constance over to Azel and helped her to mount. "I was planning on restocking our food supply in town last night."

Azel slipped her fingers into Constance's mane, gently rubbing the horse's neck.

That small motion distracted Erich. He had noticed Azel consistently did small things to care for Constance, but he hadn't stopped to think about it. He'd seen plenty of his fellow guardsmen treat their mounts as nothing more than pack animals. Not surprisingly, those were the same men whose actions became more aggressive when they wore their gray uniforms.

Azel—the sorceress who had taken human life without a thought—took extra care to ease the burden of the animal she was riding. She had also kindly gone out of her way to wake Erich from his nightmares, even hurting herself in the process.

Something did not add up about this girl.

He looked up at her, wishing she could speak to him and explain what was going on.

Her eyebrows were raised, and she rubbed a hand across her stomach.

"Oh, right," Erich said. "I got distracted for a second. We have enough food for a little while longer. There's another town on the border of Iseldis, just before the mountain pass. If we push ourselves, we can make it there in three days."

Azel patted Constance's neck with a question in her eyes. "What about the horses?" she seemed to be saying.

"The horses will be fine," Erich answered. "They're used to traveling, and they've been happily eating all this new greenreign growth. Besides, you're so small Constance probably doesn't even know you're on top of her."

Azel nodded, her expression relieved.

Turning to mount his horse, Erich felt even more confused. This girl was no killer. He could still hear the words of the townspeople in that tavern echoing through his head. Their ludicrous accusations haunted him. He had thought—and said—similar things. But they didn't know Azel, and he did. He was beginning to, at least.

As they made their way back to the main trail, he rode slightly behind her, studying her with new eyes.

Her shoulders were slim, even buried beneath the blanket she kept wrapped around herself while the air was still cold. Her hair hung loose around her shoulders, its jumbled curls both tangled and smooth. Her skin was lighter than his, lighter than most people's he knew in Iseldis. The freckles that danced over her nose and cheeks were the cutest thing he had ever seen.

Frankly, she was beautiful. Not in an elegant, seductive

way as the councilor had warned him—but in a bright, earthy way.

He rode up beside her. Even if she couldn't talk, they had still managed to have a few interesting conversations.

"What is the one thing you wish you could do right now if nothing stood in your way?" Erich asked.

She made a motion of splashing water on her face and then rubbing her skin.

"Bathe?" Erich guessed. "I couldn't agree more. You need it."

Her eyes went wide, and she opened her mouth in a mocking expression of shock.

"I was only jesting!" Erich said, even though he knew she was teasing.

She pointed at him, then pinched her nose closed. "You stink."

Erich grinned. "A hot bath does sound amazing right now, doesn't it?"

They rode hard over the next few days, arriving on the outskirts of the town Erich had mentioned in the afternoon of the third day.

Before they rode in, Erich switched back to his gray uniform. "Let's keep a lower profile this time," he explained. "We can just ride in, find a few merchants, purchase some fresh food, and get out. How does that sound?"

Azel nodded. She didn't look excited, but she did agree. She rearranged the blanket around her shoulders, hugging it high up her neck to hide the bright white necklace.

"Good idea," Erich commented. "This will be fine. I won't leave your side."

She nodded again, although she still did not seem completely convinced.

The town was small, but several market booths lined its main plaza. As the last outpost before the mountain pass, these villagers were always ready to sell provisions to passing travelers.

Azel remained seated on Constance and Erich in front of them, leading his horse. He went to a few stalls to gather more cheeses, meats, and bread.

Azel remained quiet—as usual—but Erich noticed her eyes keeping a constant watch on the sleepy town around them.

When she wasn't looking at him, he bartered with a merchant for a few extra items.

A short time later, they were back on the open road.

"That went well," Erich said. He patted the plump saddlebag behind him. "We'll eat like kings for the next few days."

Azel had loosened the blanket, letting it fall back down to her waist in the late afternoon sun.

Seeing her relax eased a tension Erich hadn't realized he was holding.

He couldn't help but notice her simple brown dress was in dire need of . . . nothing. What it needed was to be thrown out and never worn again. He smiled. "Let's stop early tonight. I think everyone is tired and deserves a rest."

Azel nodded with a smile, giving Constance another neck rub.

Veering off the trail, Erich found a good spot for camping. As always, he looked for an area with clean running water for the horses.

"How's your foot?" Erich asked as he lifted Azel from Constance.

Azel grimaced, shaking her head.

"Do you want to sit by the stream and soak it in the cool water?"

"*Yes!*" Azel mouthed the word with such conviction that Erich laughed.

He carried her to the most comfortable spot he could see and gently set her on the ground. While she dipped her foot in the water, Erich went back to his saddlebags.

CHAPTER 26

*A*izel felt a tingle run down her spine as the icy water of the stream enveloped her foot. It instantly soothed the burning sensation in her ankle, and she welcomed its numbing effect.

Her injury was finally starting to heal, but it still felt sore.

A bright orange blob caught her eye. It looked like a tiny tree, growing from the mossy ground next to her. Reaching out, she poked it gently. It was firm but light. The rounded orange top was dotted with small cream spots, and its mini trunk appeared to be the same cream color.

Now that she'd noticed it, she saw dozens of them scattered around her.

Delighted, she pinched the one closest to her, gently wiggling its base free from the ground. It wasn't quite like a plant; it was almost like a hardened foam, or a sea creature. The entire thing was smaller than the palm of her hand. She loved it.

"I don't have any hot water," Erich said behind her. "But I do have this." He crouched next to her, holding out a bar of soap.

She held out her hand with a smile.

"You found a mushroom," Erich said, identifying the miniature tree.

"Mushroom." She repeated the word to herself. This was a good name for the funny plant.

"Want me to put it in your sack for you?" Erich asked.

Aizel nodded, handing him her treasure. She had taken the sack from her waist and placed it in Constance's saddlebag for safekeeping.

"It might not dry out very well," Erich commented as he walked toward the horses. "But there are plenty all over the mountain. They come in a few different colors, too."

He opened her sack and gently deposited the mushroom into it.

Aizel picked another from the ground to continue studying its plump little shape.

"What's this?" Erich asked.

She turned back.

He was holding her mother's pearl vial up to his nose.

Aizel froze, her whole body tensing. *Put that down!* she yelled in her head. *It's dangerous!* She shook her head frantically, waving her arms to get his attention.

He didn't notice her.

She took her ankle out of the water, pulling herself up into a kneeling position.

"It's beautiful." Erich closed the lid and dropped the vial back into her sack, leaving the horses. "Is that Istroyan craftsmanship?"

Aizel nodded, relief flooding through her.

"The hammered pearl is elegantly wrought," he said. "And that lotus scent . . . it reminds me . . . never mind."

"Reminds you of what?" Aizel wanted to ask. *"That time I saved your life by using its magic so you could breathe?"*

Erich returned to her side. "Now, about that bath you were dreaming of earlier." He crouched in front of her again, balancing on his toes as he held out the bar of soap.

She looked from his hand to his eyes, her smile fueled by relief and excitement. Cold water or not, she was going to get clean tonight.

Grabbing the bar from his hand, she lifted it to her nose. It smelled fresh. It was not scented with anything she recognized; it was just mild and sweet.

She held it back out to him. *"You first?"*

"Oh, no." Erich pushed her hand back. "You need it more than I do."

Aizel narrowed her eyes at the teasing boy in front of her. Two could play at that game.

"You first." Reaching out, she playfully shoved him into the stream.

Balanced as he was over his toes, he toppled over, landing in the shallow water with a splash.

Aizel laughed soundlessly, swishing the bar of soap in the water while she waited for him to resurface.

At its deepest, the water was perhaps as high as her knees. Erich's head was under the surface where he'd fallen.

He wasn't moving.

Alarmed, she watched him for a moment longer.

He reached a single hand out of the water.

She relaxed. He was still toying with her. But he was taking an awfully long time about it.

His hand fell back under the water. It was a stiff,

awkward motion. She couldn't see his face clearly, but bubbles rose from his mouth.

Something was not right.

Still on her knees, she crawled into the water. Grabbing his arm, she yanked him back up into a sitting position.

His head resurfaced, a look of absolute terror on his face. He sat there for a moment, gasping for air, then scrambled out of the stream as fast as he could.

Aizel followed him—a little more slowly—to the mossy riverbank. *"What's wrong?"* She reached out, touching his knee.

He shook his head, avoiding her eyes. "I . . . I can't. I . . . water. I can't do water. It terrifies me still. It . . ."

Suddenly, everything fell into place. Aizel tilted her head into her open palm. *"Your nightmares? You're afraid of water even while you are awake?"*

Erich nodded, looking down. "Yes, the nightmares are always about water, too."

"I'm sorry," Aizel mouthed.

"It's my fault," Erich said. "I was teasing you first. Why don't you enjoy that soap and I'll go get us a fire going? We'll both need to dry off soon."

Aizel nodded. He seemed as though he wanted some space.

Sitting on the edge of the stream, she did her best to wash her face, hands, and feet. Her hair was already wet, but it was too tangled to resubmerge long enough in the chilly water for a proper washing.

She felt much better by the time Erich had lit a small fire.

Crawling to join him, she sat as close as she dared to the welcome heat. *"Want to talk about it?"* She raised her eyebrows at him.

Erich blew on the burning flames, coaxing them to grow larger. "Ever since that day at sea . . ." His eyes remained on the fire. "I would have drowned that day. I remember rope around my arm, dragging me down." He paused, his body trembling for a brief moment. "I think someone swam down after me . . ."

Aizel nodded, encouraging him to continue. Had he recalled her being there?

He narrowed his eyes at her for a moment before continuing. "Water terrifies me now. It attacks me in my dreams." He smiled sheepishly. "I know that sounds ridiculous."

She shook her head. *"No, it doesn't."*

He jumped up. "I almost forgot. I found something else in town today." Opening his saddlebag, he took off his wet gray jacket and slipped back into his colorful purple doublet. He topped off his outfit with the feathered cap.

When he turned back toward her, his face was lighter. He had either forgotten about his scare in the water or chosen not to think about it.

He walked around to her side of the fire, shaking out a folded bundle of fabric. "This is all they had, but I thought you could use it." He was holding a cream shirt and loose black pants. "You don't have to take them if you don't like them."

Aizel tapped her chin, pretending to consider his offer. She desperately wanted to change out of her damp, cold, dirty dress. The woolen shirt and comfortable pants looked clean and fresh. She didn't care that they were boy's clothing.

"He didn't have a dress or anything, or I would have gotten that." Erich's voice was hesitant.

She looked past the outstretched items into the nervous face of the young man holding them. He had been scrupulously kind to her since that night at the tavern. She hadn't missed the confused glances he'd been throwing her way when he thought she wasn't looking.

His black hair faded into the evening light, but she could still make out the soft waves that flowed over his ears. His brown eyes reflected the light of the fire. They were kind, filled with concern for her and fear he had done the wrong thing. His tall shoulders sloped downward, relaxed in his comfortable, preferred clothing.

Suddenly, she was no longer cold.

"Never mind," he said, looking away from her intense scrutiny.

She shook her head. *"Come closer."* She beckoned him down with her hand. She wanted him to feel less terrified, and she had a feeling that doing something humorous would help distract his mind.

"What do you need?" he asked, leaning down toward her.

"This." She reached up to take the clothing from his hand, but with an extra stretch she reached higher and grabbed the hat from his head.

With a satisfied grin, she settled it onto her head.

His jaw opened in surprise, and then he pinched his lips together. "Fine. I see how it is."

Pulling the long feather down in front of her face, she admired its vibrant color. She refocused her eyes from the feather to its owner.

"Actually, it looks rather good on you," he said.

She grinned in response.

He turned to leave, but she grabbed the new clothes from his hand as well.

"Thank you," she mouthed.

He returned to his side of the fire. "If I find you another feather as good as this one, can I have my hat back?" he asked.

She shrugged. *"Maybe."*

CHAPTER 27

When Erich helped her to the ground four days later, Aizel didn't release her grip on him. Instead, she squeezed her hand on his arm to let him know she wanted to try something new.

He paused while she slowly pulled herself onto her feet, using his arm to steady herself.

Her ankle had felt much better for the last two days, but she hadn't tried to put any weight on it.

"Careful," Erich said upon realizing what she was attempting.

She nodded and slowly pressed the toes of her hurt foot into the ground. It was not the same as putting weight on it; she was just testing out her pain threshold without going too far. Her ankle felt stiff but otherwise fine.

Pressing down with her knee, she tried putting some weight on it.

It held up.

She inhaled in relief and removed her hand from Erich's arm.

He remained exactly where he was, holding his arms out right next to her, ready to catch her if she fell.

His concern was endearing, but she pushed his hands away. She wasn't going to break. Taking a tentative step forward, she slowly rolled her weight across her bad foot.

That caused a little pain. However, if she lifted her foot without bending her ankle, perhaps she could support her weight with the bones of her ankle instead of the hurting muscle.

Hobbling forward, she tested out her theory. She could only walk forward a few steps since dense undergrowth surrounded the open patch of moss they had stopped in.

By her fifth step, she was facing a wall of ferns, so she turned back to Erich. She had her mobility again, and it felt like a piece of herself was back under control. She held up her arms in triumph.

Erich smiled at her, his boyish face looking innocent and happy with the biggest grin she had ever seen.

His joy fueled her own, and she smiled back.

"Finally." He rolled his eyes dramatically. "I was getting tired of carting you around everywhere." His words were clearly meant as a jest. His smile remained and his eyes sparkled, even in the dimming light.

Aizel raised her eyebrows. She used her hand to mimic a person speaking then pointed to Constance. *Tell that to the horse.*

He threw back his head and laughed. "Fine, you're right. Poor Constance has done most of the carting around here, hasn't she?"

Aizel grinned back at him. She felt so . . . light. Their

conversing was nearly effortless.

Hobbling around the small clearing, she helped Erich prepare the fire and roast some dried meat.

Sitting across from him in the growing darkness, Aizel soaked in the gentle sounds of the crackling fire and Erich's voice. Leaves rustled overhead, and the occasional call of a night bird sang through the sky.

The sounds worked together harmoniously, even with the happy tenor of Erich's voice mixed in with it all.

She had stopped paying attention to what he was saying. Occasional words and phrases like "dancing" and "sneaking through the hall" registered in her mind.

She listened instead to the silent peacefulness of the moment around her. If only they could stay here forever and she didn't have to carry out the young king's plan and murder Erich and . . .

Her stomach turned. Suddenly, the fire felt too hot, the forest sounded too ominous, and Erich's voice was too loud.

"I don't think anyone has ever listened to me so intently before, Azel."

"It's Aizel," she corrected him for the umpteenth time in her head, feeling guilty that she had absolutely no idea what he'd just been saying.

"I just wanted to let you know that I appreciate that."

Aizel looked up at him with a pretend smile on her face, but he was staring down at the fire, his hands gesturing in rhythm with his voice.

"As I was saying," he continued.

Aizel watched his hands, fully intending to actually listen to him this time, when a crack in the ferns to her right redirected her attention. Was that the sound of something trampling through the woods toward them?

She held a finger up to her lips, urging Erich to be quiet for a moment. It was probably just a nocturnal animal roaming through the forest. Hopefully, it was a small one.

He didn't notice her motion at all, entrenched as he was in . . . whatever he was saying.

Aizel sat still, trying to listen for any more sounds above the noise of his voice.

There it was again, accompanied by a high-pitched metallic clink. No animal could make that sound.

Aizel waved her arms frantically, hoping to draw Erich's attention. *"Be quiet! Something's out there!"* The words formed in her mouth but never came out.

The footsteps grew closer.

Forcing air through her teeth, she made a hissing noise.

That finally got his attention.

He looked up, a question in his eyes, but it was too late to explain anything to him. She shook her head quickly.

Wrapping the blanket around her shoulders, she threw herself to the ground and rolled backward under the arched branches of a bushy fern.

She saw Erich scan the area around him, but by the time he was on his feet, five cloaked figures had poured into the small space and surrounded him.

Erich took a step back only to collide with one of the men he hadn't seen behind him.

Aizel ran her hands over the ground around her as quietly as she could, searching for something she could use to protect herself if need be. She didn't know if they had seen her before they'd rushed into the glade or if she was truly hidden. Her fingers found nothing but dirt and soft, rotting sticks.

"Hello, traveler," one of the hooded figures said. "You

wouldn't happen to have any coin to spare for a few poor farmers who are down on their luck?"

"Coin?" Erich's voice squeaked.

Thanks to the light of the fire at his feet, Aizel could see his eyes as he took in the hooded figures surrounding him. He threw a glance at her hiding place but then looked away. "How much would it take to satisfy you, friends?" He reached into his pocket and pulled out three coins, dropping them into the stranger's hand.

"Who was you talking to just now?" another bandit asked.

"Myself," Erich answered without a second's hesitation. "It gets awful lonely traveling . . . alone."

Aizel sent him a silent prayer of gratitude. He had no reason to protect her, but he consistently did. A small flicker caught her attention.

Sparkles of pink and purple shone near her head, reflecting the light of the fire. Corundum! Or was it carborundum? Either way, it could be a weapon.

Reaching toward it, she began to pry it from the dirt.

"Where are you traveling to?" the first bandit questioned. He had pocketed the coins, but his other hand held a knife. It was pointed at Erich.

"To the White Palace. To speak with King Gareth."

The man holding the knife bent forward, laughing. "You hear that, fellows? He thinks he's going to see King Gareth, but he only has three coins to share with his fellow mates." He stood abruptly, bringing the knife even closer to Erich.

Aizel wanted to slap her forehead. He could blithely lie about being alone, but he couldn't think of a better excuse than to be traveling to the biggest capital on the continent.

"We don't want to harm you, friend," said the man with the knife. "Do we, fellows?"

A chorus of voices affirmed his words. "No, no. We hate harming folks."

"We avoid it at all when possible," a woman's voice pitched in.

"Much rather share some coin than harm a man." Their voices combined were an odd mix of happy and regretful over an action they hadn't even committed yet.

The tension in the small glade squeezed its way into Aizel's lungs.

She watched as the leader dropped his knife hand and pointed the small blade toward the ground. He leaned back on the balls of his feet, giving himself more room to spread his arms.

The carborundum finally wiggled loose from the packed dirt. Aizel gripped it tightly.

"Don't make us hurt you." The man practically begged. "We hate to see it happen to a good fellow such as yourself, but what is one supposed to do?"

For a brief moment, Aizel held her breath, wondering if this was the perfect answer to her problem. If she sat back and did nothing, these bandits would take care of Erich for her and she wouldn't have to murder him.

She could still report back to the king, but she wouldn't have to do the horrifying deed herself.

"I've been traveling for quite some time now, and my reserves are running dry," Erich said, licking his lips. Aizel could see the fear in his eyes.

The leader of the bandits slumped his shoulders in defeat, shaking his head. "I told you we didn't want to do this, but you are giving us no choice, my friend. Do we have a choice, fellows?"

Again, the chorus of affirming words rose around the campfire.

"You said it, boss."

"He ain't leaving us no choice."

"It's downright terrible, it is." The final voice definitely belonged to a woman, but Aizel couldn't tell which one she was.

The leader's blade flashed in the light of the flames as he casually brought it to rest against Erich's collarbone.

"You . . . you could consider not doing it this one time, perhaps?" Erich offered. His skin was beginning to look shiny.

Aizel held herself in place. If she waited just a few more moments, her problem would be solved. Well, one of her problems would be solved—the most immediate one.

"I'm terribly sorry, friend." The leader clamped his other hand around the back of Erich's neck and stepped aside so he could guide the prince toward the fire.

Aizel closed her eyes, unable to watch what would happen next.

"This is really very upsetting," the leader continued. "To all of us."

"Myself included," Erich said, his typical dry humor coming out as though it might defuse the situation.

The leader laughed, slapping Erich on the back.

Aizel exhaled, anger and frustration filling her as she rolled out of her hiding spot. She couldn't stand idly by while Erich was hurt—or worse—by a bunch of crazed bandits.

Clutching the rock in her raised hand, she hobbled forward, making as much noise as she could.

The leader instantly turned his attention from Erich to her, as did the rest of the bandits.

She crouched down, holding the rock out in front of her before the two bandits closest to her could pounce on her.

The leader's face broke into a grin. "Another lovely addition to the party. What a lucky bunch of lads we are tonight! Not one but two travelers!"

"We have some food," Erich cried. "It's in the saddlebag. You can help yourself to it."

"What a generous offer." The leader slapped Erich's back. "Check the bags, fellows. And remember what Robin said. No more than half."

Aizel stood up straight, dropping the rock slightly. *Robin?* she wanted to call out. Could it be the same Robin?

"Look at his fancy clothes," one of the bandits complained. "All of this is less than half of what they have back at their fancy houses."

The leader shook his head. "Nobody here disrespects Robin or they are out on their own. That is final, and you all know it. No more than half."

Aizel knew it might be futile, but she couldn't let this chance go. She boldly stepped forward, hobbling over her bad foot until she stood next to the fire, opposite Erich and the leader. As she had hoped, the leader turned toward her.

The man smiled at her warmly. It thoroughly confused Aizel since he was still holding a knife to Erich's throat. Somehow, his smile seemed genuine. "Never fear, little lady," he said. "We won't be doing anything we don't have to tonight."

Her mind raced through the possible ways she could use her hands to speak the words she needed. She dropped the rock in her hand.

Hooking her thumbs together, she flapped her hands through the air to imitate a bird.

The man looked confused.

She pointed to her mouth and shook her head.

"Oh, you can't speak?"

She nodded quickly, then repeated the flapping motion with her hand.

He watched her hands very closely, but his expression remained confused. "Are you trying to tell me something?"

She nodded again.

"Help me figure this out, fellows," he called to his men.

"It's a bird," Erich said.

"Not you," the leader said, his voice dropping in pitch. "I didn't ask for your help, now did I?" Turning back to Aizel, he asked, "Is it a bird?"

She nodded. She repeated the bird motion, then pointed to the bandit leader.

"Me?" he asked.

With a sigh of exasperation, she repeated the two motions.

"Take your time, little lady. We'll figure this out," he said.

Aizel couldn't help the small smile that flitted across her face. She hadn't expected a bandit to be patient.

"She thinks you're a bird, boss," one of the bandits called out.

The leader burst into a loud laugh. "I'm no bird, lady, but I have always wished I could fly."

Aizel wanted to stomp her foot and yell her words. *Do you know Robin Lockwood?!"* she screamed in her head. How else could she ask that?

Lockwood.

She could work with that.

Scanning the area, she bent down and picked up a piece of soft wood from the ground near the fire.

She pointed toward the leader's belt, where a small ring of keys hung on his hip.

He followed her gaze and placed his hand on the jangling implements. "Keys?"

She nodded, then made a motion with her hand as though unlocking something.

"Keys twist?"

She kept repeating the motion, looking around at the group of bandits to see if anyone else understood.

"Unlock," Erich muttered.

"Quiet," the bandit leader snapped under his breath. Then, louder, as though no one else had heard that, he said, "Unlocking something?"

Nodding, she reversed the motion.

"Locking something?"

She nodded, smiling brightly. Then she held up the piece of wood.

"Tree?"

She shook her head.

"Wood?"

Nodding again, she made the locking motion and then indicated the wood.

When the leader said nothing, she stopped moving and stared at him expectantly. This was his chance to put it all together.

"Keys. Locking. Wood." He said the words slowly, trying to make sense of them.

She nodded, encouraging him to say the words again.

"Keys. Locking. Wood."

Aizel turned to Erich, hoping he might have understood, but his face was scrunched in concentration. She could see him mouthing the words. "Lock. Wood."

She grabbed at the jewel around her neck, yanking against it although she knew it would do no good. *"Robin Lockwood!"* she screamed in her head.

"Your necklace," the bandit leader continued, as though her actions were still part of the game. "Wait . . . that necklace looks familiar." His hands tapped the air as his mind connected the clues she had given him. "Bird. Lock. Wood. Robin Lockwood!"

Aizel clapped her hands together.

"You're a friend of Robin's? Well, why didn't you say so!" The bandit leader slipped his knife back into a leather case at his belt. "What about him?" He indicated toward Erich with his thumb.

Aizel had momentarily forgotten about Erich. He didn't look as relieved as she thought he would. Rather, his face was unreadable. His eyes looked confused, and he kept glancing between her and the bandit leader.

Aizel nodded, hoping her vote of confidence would vouch for Erich.

The bandit leader exhaled loudly, his shoulders dropping as his whole body relaxed. "Do you have any idea how relieved I am? Sometimes, I really hate what I do."

Aizel thought he might have more control over that than he let on, but she didn't push the matter. She had other things to communicate while she still had the bandit leader's attention.

She flapped her hands again like a bird, then raised her palms in a questioning gesture. *"Where's Robin?"*

But the bandit leader was still piecing together the clues he had received. "If you're wearing one of those necklaces . . . doesn't that mean you're a Majis?"

CHAPTER 28

$\mathcal{E}$rich tensed.

Azel had just saved his life by risking her own.

And now that these bandits had figured she was a Majis—he wasn't about to let her get hurt.

Jumping away from the bandit leader, Erich took a wide step around the fire to stand at her side. He was still confused about who and what she was, but if she was going to face justice, it wouldn't be at the hands of an angry mob.

Azel stared across the fire at the bandit leader. She slowly lifted her head, pausing for a moment before nodding once to answer his question.

"No!" Erich yelled. "It's just a necklace that looks like any other necklace."

Ignoring him, the bandit leader reached up and dropped his hood, giving them a clear view of his face for the first time.

Despite his unruly facial hair and weathered skin, the man's face appeared open and relaxed. His eyes traveled up and down Azel, and there was respect—perhaps even awe—in his gaze. "I've always wanted to meet a Majis." He held out his right hand, palm up. "May I?"

Azel's face was so confused, Erich would have laughed if the moment were any less tense. She tentatively raised her hand palm up, holding it in the air in front of her as if unsure what he was indicating.

The bandit wrapped his hand around hers and twisted her wrist as he bowed low over it, kissing the back of her fingers. "My lady, if there is any way I may be of service to you and your people in your fight for freedom, you have my aid."

Erich couldn't comprehend what was happening. Not only was this bandit not afraid of a Majis, he was also acting as though they were the ones who needed help. Didn't he know what was going on in this war?

"Count me in," the lady bandit's voice called out, adding her support to their leader's.

"And me as well."

"Aye. We've always helped the underdog, that we have." The words of support came from all around the small fire.

Erich turned to Azel to see her reaction.

Her normally guarded face was filled with emotion. The look of appreciation in her eyes stabbed him to the core. He felt left out.

He turned back to the bandit, wanting to see what it was about this rural outlaw that moved her so.

But the rural outlaw in question had straightened his back and was wearing a very different expression on his face. He was still grasping Azel's hand protectively, but he glared at Erich with a distrustful fury. "Who is he, and what are you doing with him?"

Erich's eyes went wide. He was about to hand her over to the Council—and their magical examiners—in less than two days. He held up his hands in defense. "I . . . I am . . ." He struggled to find the words to explain himself.

The bandit leader pulled Azel around the fire, moving her away from Erich and into the safety of his group. The fingers of his other hand curled around the hilt of his dagger.

"I would never hurt her!" Erich spoke the only truth he could think of at the moment, but it sounded like an excuse even to his own ears.

The leader leaned closer. "You're clearly not one of them. What is a rich quotidian fool like yourself doing alone in the woods with a muted Majis, and why haven't you removed her necklace? You're not one of those Chendas secret soldiers, are you?" His eyes looked over Erich as if expecting the answer to his questions to make itself apparent. "Search that saddlebag again and see if he has one of those fancy doublets the military boys wear."

Erich shook his head. The man had discovered all their truths, and he could think of no way to talk himself out of this.

Could he talk himself out of this?

Did he even want to?

If this bandit figured out what was going on and whisked Azel away, he wouldn't have to deliver her to King Gareth.

Erich had been acting in his kingdom's best interest, but over the last few days, he'd come to the conclusion that not everything was as clear as he'd understood it to be. Azel was not at all who he'd thought she was, and he realized he would be more than relieved to see her go free.

Azel grabbed the leader's arm, pulling him toward her and shaking her head.

The bandit looked down at her, his eyes questioning.

Azel stepped around the fire and slid her hand into Erich's arm, hugging herself to his side possessively.

She shook her head, her meaning clear.

"I still don't trust him," the bandit leader responded. "But I won't hurt him if that's what you want."

Azel nodded, gracing the outlaw with a dazzling smile.

Erich felt another pang of jealousy. She had never given him a smile like that. Not that he'd done anything to deserve it.

"But that still don't answer the question. What are you doing out here?" The bandit's question was directed at Erich.

He quickly looked down at Azel, not sure how he could answer the question other than with the truth.

Azel repeated the bird motion with her hands, following it up by spreading both palms wide and shrugging her shoulders in a question. Her eyes darted around the area as though she were looking for something. *Where's Robin?*

"We are looking for Robin Lockwood."

She squeezed his arm affirmingly.

"You need Robin's help?" the bandit asked.

Azel nodded.

"See, that's tricky." The man leaned back on his heels and stroked his beard. "She can be awfully hard to find, even for those of us lucky to call her friend. Of course, for you, she wouldn't mind if I told you where she is. And I would, but the problem is I don't know."

Erich felt Azel's arm go slack. He looked down, catching the disappointment on her face. "Could you let her know that we are looking for her if you see her soon?" he asked.

Azel smiled up at him.

The bandit's eyes opened wide. "I could do that. I'll tell

her you're headed for Chendas. Which . . . you might be in luck and find her first. She's been spending a lot of time there these days, what with everything that's going on."

Erich had no idea what was going on in Chendas, but he didn't dare to ask.

"You folks have a safe trip," the bandit said. "Never know who you're going to run into out here."

With a nod of his head, the bandit disappeared into the ferns along with the rest of his troupe.

Erich wrapped his arm around Azel's shoulders and pulled her close.

The following morning, they were on their way as early as possible. Though the bandits had ended up being harmless, Aizel could sense that Erich was eager to get as far away from them as possible.

"This is officially the border into Chendas," Erich said. They had crossed the mountain pass and were beginning their descent on the other side of the mountain range.

She only had two more days—maybe three—before they would arrive at the marble palace.

Three more days to either murder the young man whom she had grown to grudgingly respect or find a new way to free her sister.

They were riding side by side, and she glanced furtively at Erich. He, too, seemed less animated than before. Maybe he was dreading the end of their journey as well.

"Let's stop early tonight," Erich said, confirming her suspicions. "Constance is looking pretty tired."

Aizel looked down at her horse. The spotted mare was

prancing down the road like she hadn't a care in the world. She didn't look tired at all.

But Aizel was completely happy to extend their trip, so she nodded her assent.

"Besides, there's a beautiful spot I discovered close to here that would be especially good for watching the sunset," Erich continued. "And, if I recall correctly, it had lots of flowers."

Aizel smiled, raising her eyebrows as she nodded again. *"I already agreed, silly boy. You don't have to convince me twice."*

A short distance later, Erich nudged his horse onto a small side path, and Aizel followed his lead. Her heart felt squeezed, like it couldn't beat properly. She didn't want this trip to end, and it hurt even more to know Erich didn't want it to end either.

But the thought of her sister in the hands of the ruthless Quotidian . . . anger welled up inside her at the impossible choice she had been given. Why did Erich deserve to live while her sister died? He was a prince! He had lived a happy life with a loving family and complete freedom already. Didn't Celesta deserve to experience the same thing while she was still alive?

The intensity of her feelings overwhelmed Aizel, and she didn't notice the changing landscape around her.

"What do you think?" Erich cut into her thoughts.

Aizel lifted her head. They were riding through a large, grassy plain. Trees lined the horizon, and she could see a gentle river bubbling quietly through the grass.

It was beautiful. She lifted her eyebrows and nodded at Erich.

"It's beautiful, isn't it?" he said as though reading her

mind. "The only problem with it is that it belongs to Chendas and not Iseldis. This isn't all of it, though."

Carefully guiding the horses over the uneven ground, Erich followed the side of the small river.

The water was so clear Aizel could see every rounded pebble on the bottom of the riverbed. Watching the constant motion was mesmerizing.

As they approached the end of the meadow, she could see that the edge was a drop-off. The sounds of rushing water grew louder as the river poured over a cliffside to create a cascading waterfall.

Erich dismounted, and she followed his lead. Leaving the horses to drink from the stream, he reached for her hand and pulled her toward the edge of the cliff.

"I found this place a few weeks ago when I was searching for you," he said. "It's surprisingly uninhabited for being so close to the capital. I'm amazed no one has discovered it and built a small farm here. I would be quite happy to wake up to this view every day."

Aizel opened her mouth in amazement as they came close enough to the cliff's edge to see the views below.

This had to be the very top of the world.

The small river turned into a foaming white waterfall. It bounced and sprayed down the cliffside, which was taller than the treetops below it. A series of interconnected lakes spread out across the landscape below, offsetting the deep green forests with a bright blue.

In all her life, she had never seen anything more beautiful than the ocean. While that still held true, the deeply saturated colors of this endless view were a possible rival.

"It's incredible, isn't it?"

Aizel barely registered his words. Such an obvious question hardly deserved an answer.

"Have you never seen it before?" he questioned further. "I received a report that you had been sighted at a village just through that forest. By the time I got there, I could find no trace of a wandering Majis sorceress. I thought you might have left the village in this direction."

Thoroughly confused, Aizel looked up at him. She had no idea what he was talking about. His voice was odd, like he was lying. What was going on? She shook her head and swiped her hand through the air. *What are you talking about?* She pointed to herself, then to the ground at her feet, then to all the land in view. Then she shook her head again. *I've never been anywhere near here at all.*

Erich watched her, his face puzzled. He turned back to look at the valley far below.

For the briefest moment, Aizel realized she could carry out her task here and now. They were standing on the edge of a tall cliff in an empty meadow, and he had his back to her. A life for a life. Justice.

She could imagine her arms lifting . . .

She jumped backward, putting physical distance between herself and Erich.

This wasn't her. Those thoughts weren't her own. She was tired and scared and felt like she had no option available to her.

But she did. She did have the option to choose not to commit a horrible act of violence that would end the life of another person. The Quotidian might stoop to that level of evil, but she never would.

Her skin tingled as the knowledge of that control flowed through her body. She felt strong and alive, like she had all those days ago when she'd dove into the freezing sea in the middle of the night.

She didn't know how this would play out, but she would decide what she did from here out. No one else would be making those choices for her.

She was strong. Stronger than most anyone else she knew.

Her entire life had been spent facing the wrong side of injustice, and she wasn't weaker for it. She was fierce now, and more resilient.

Erich turned around. He must have noticed her jumping back. "Do tall spaces frighten you?" His face held concern. "I'm sorry, I didn't know."

She smiled at him, accepting his kind words fully now that her heart was no longer conflicted.

His eyes lit up at her smile. "Your hair is stunning in the sunlight," he said. "I thought it was brown at first, but now I can't ever seem to stop staring at it. I've never seen such a beautiful shade of red anywhere."

"*Thank you,*" Aizel mouthed. Her throat felt clogged, but whether it was from the words stuck in her chest or from the kindness in his voice, she couldn't tell.

"Azel." He stepped closer to her until he was standing directly in front of her. "Something the bandit said last night has been on my mind."

She raised her eyebrows at him.

His dark brown eyes glanced between hers, his face earnest and serious. "He asked why I hadn't removed your necklace." Erich held out his finger to point to the gem on her throat, though he didn't quite touch it. "Can I do that?" His voice was lower than she had ever heard it.

Keeping her eyes on his, she nodded.

"Can you remove it?"

She shook her head, reaching up behind her neck to demonstrate. Though it was tied in a simple bow, she couldn't undo it.

As she fiddled with it, the ribbon pulled tighter around her throat, pinching into her skin. She stopped, dropping her hands and breathing slowly to offset the hallmark of Quotidian magic: pain.

Erich reached up and gently touched the side of the ribbon. "Is it spelled? So you cannot take it off but others can?"

She nodded.

"Even if I do not have magic?"

She nodded again. Her heart continued pounding. This time, it wasn't from the Quotidian magic but from the understanding of what he was asking. Erich wanted to give her voice back. He was trusting her enough to do so. *"Take it off,"* she pleaded with her eyes. *"Let me speak with you. Let me tell you what I know. Then you can tell me why the Quotidian king wants you dead."*

"If I release this . . ." His fingers slid further behind her neck, touching the knot itself. ". . . you will have access to your magic through your voice."

The words he spoke were obvious, but the tone behind them seemed to ask whether it was safe to free her.

He was standing so close she had to tilt her head backward to look up at him. She nodded, assuring him with complete honesty that she would do nothing to harm him. She had never used her magic for harm before, and she never intended to.

CHAPTER 30

$\mathcal{E}$rich looked down into the green eyes of the young woman before him. He was surrounded by deep evergreen trees, bright green grass, and the emerald shimmer of the lakes far below. But the soft hazel green of her eyes had his full attention.

If he removed her necklace—with its murky green jewel —he would be placing himself at her mercy.

But hadn't he been at her mercy the night before, when she'd risked her life to save him from the bandits?

Everything about her was innocent.

He didn't know what to believe, for the girl in front of him didn't seem capable of the attack he had witnessed at sea. She had tried to share things with him multiple times, and he felt she had something she wanted to say. But no one was listening because no one could hear her.

That simple fact alone filled his heart with empathy. He knew the deep loneliness of being unheard.

He had two choices. He could let things stand as they were. Tomorrow, he could ride with her into Chendas and deliver her to King Gareth and his Council. It was the safe choice, the responsible choice. It was the choice Ian would have made.

Or, he could move his fingers and untie the bright white ribbon around her neck. He could give this girl her voice back and listen to what she had to say.

He had a feeling her words might upset his entire world. But at this point, he knew there was only one clear option for him.

Too many things weren't making sense, and a person who had some of the answers was standing right in front of him.

All he had to do was listen.

Gazing into her eyes, he let out a shaky breath and reached for the ribbon.

Her neck was soft and warm under his fingers, but he ignored the tingling sensation that crept up his arm at the contact.

He easily found the knot in the ribbon, and his fingers worked to loosen it. Unable to see it, he leaned over her shoulder, bringing his face close to hers.

Her eyes fluttered closed. She was standing motionless, encased in the circle of his arms. She kept so still, Erich couldn't even hear her breathe.

Finally, his clumsy fingers found the right loop, and he tugged the ribbon free.

The white strands fluttered open and slipped over her shoulders, pulled as they were by the weight of the jewel. Instinctively, he reached up, grabbing the green gem before it fell. He pulled the spelled necklace away from her throat.

For the longest second he had ever experienced, she remained motionless in front of him. Then she exhaled the breath she had been holding with a long, deep sigh.

Tilting her head back up to look into his eyes, she opened her mouth. "It's Aizel," she said. "Eye-zell."

CHAPTER 31

"EYE-zell," Erich smiled as he repeated her name with the proper pronunciation. "Aizel."

The sound of her own name was surprisingly grounding. During the last few weeks, she had been called many things. None of them had been her name.

She inhaled a deep breath, the muscles in her chest loosening and expanding. "You are wrong, Erich, prince of whatever Quotidian kingdom you come from. And unless you figure that out quickly, you are going to find yourself dead. You are on the brink of a war you don't even know is happening, and you are blaming all the wrong people for what's going on."

Erich nodded in response to her rapid outburst of words. He didn't seem surprised or hurt. In fact, he was quite serious. "Was I wrong about you?"

Aizel paused for a second. Of all the things she had expected him to ask about, she was the last one. She had just said that he was going to find himself dead, and he wasn't even digging into that. She started to nod, since that had become her primary method of communication. Remembering she could talk, she practically shouted, "Yes! I have never been here before, nor was I sighted at a nearby village. I was at the white marble palace a few weeks ago, but other than that I have never been anywhere on this continent. I didn't kill your men during that shipwreck. That was the Quotidian, but I don't expect you to believe me. I was there, though, which may make it difficult to prove my innocence. But I was the one who dragged you from the depths when you were caught in the rigging of the mast that was pulling you down into the sea. So, if anything, you should be thanking me for saving your life. You're welcome." She stopped to take a breath. It felt so good to speak again. She felt as though she had so many layers and layers of words piled up inside of her that she would need the next several days to let them all out. Only then would she again be comfortable.

It was Erich's turn to do some listening anyway. She had heard enough of his ramblings to last a lifetime.

"The quotidian?" Erich asked. "What do you mean it was the quotidian? Everyone on the continent is quotidian. We can't do magic."

"Ha!" Aizel let out a short laugh. "You're jesting again?"

Erich leaned ever so slightly away from her. "No. No, I'm not. Magic has been outlawed for one thousand seasons. You —or your people—have been exiled for two hundred and fifty years. No one here can even figure out magic. The Council examiners have been attempting to unravel Majis secrets for decades, but they've found next to nothing—"

"Stop!"

Erich closed his mouth. Taking in her expression, he

relaxed his posture. "I'm sorry," he said. "I'll stop talking. Those are the things that I know, but I have a feeling you are about to tell me they aren't all correct."

She raised her eyebrows at him. *You're still talking,* she said in her mind. Then, remembering she could say it out loud, she repeated her sarcastic comment. "You're still talking."

"Right. Right." He held up his hands in defeat. "I'm listening."

"The Quotidian can definitely use magic now," Aizel continued. "I don't know when they figured it out, but they did at some point. Maybe they knew it all along." She pointed to the necklace that was still in his hand. "That is Quotidian magic."

Erich held the ribbon up, squinting at the jewel. "Is quotidian magic different?"

Aizel nodded. "Yes. The Quotidian uses pain and discord to power their spells. The Majis rely only on harmony."

"I have so many questions."

"Well, we have all night," Aizel responded. "We might as well make ourselves comfortable."

They walked back toward the horses and found a comfortable spot to sit down.

"Who do you mean when you say 'the Quotidian'?" he asked.

"Up until a few days ago, I thought it meant everyone on the continent," Aizel answered. "Now, I'm not sure. I mean, if you are a prince from one of these kingdoms and you don't even know your people can do magic . . . I don't know. That causes me concern."

Erich nodded. "Yes," he said, his voice high pitched. "I'm concerned, too."

*E*rich was glad he was sitting down. If he hadn't been, he might have fallen over from the slamming weight of the thoughts swirling in his mind. "Let's start with the people you know who can do magic."

"Use magic," Aizel corrected. "It's not something you *do*."

"Use magic," Erich repeated.

"All the Quotidian taskers can use magic," Aizel said. "That's why I thought all of you could do it, since those on the island can."

"There are quotidian people on the Isle of Exile?"

"That's what you call it? The Isle of Exile?" Aizel's expression made her look as though she had bitten something sour. "That sounds horrible."

"What do you call it?"

"Istroya," she replied. "It's the only home I've ever known. I'd hate to think my home was just called 'that place where everyone is in exile.' Although it would be a much nicer home if it didn't also have a bunch of Quotidian taskers on it, forcing us to work for them."

"Forcing you . . ." Erich's stomach turned. This was too much information all at once. "What?"

"You seriously didn't know this? What did you think we were doing in a place you called the Isle of Exile? Having a wonderful time dreaming up new spells to make other people miserable with?"

Erich averted his eyes as shame lashed through him. He'd never really thought about it. He knew—or had been told—that the Majis wouldn't leave their exile until the time was up, but he had never really thought about what they had been doing all this time. "The latter, I guess," he admitted. "We've all been assuming that you were over there feeding your anger and preparing an evil revenge."

The look of hurt in Aizel's eyes thoroughly added to the guilt he was already feeling. She shook her head in disbelief. "That would explain the way everyone's treated me since I got here."

"I am sorry about that." Erich wanted to make amends. To somehow rectify the horrible things he'd said to her and the abominable way he'd treated her—all because he had been afraid of her. The image of the bandit leader, bowing low over her hand and offering his services in honor of her freedom, came to Erich's mind. Even a lawbreaker had understood the situation better than he had.

Rolling forward, he positioned himself on one knee as a knight would do for his liege. "Aizel," he said, looking down at her face since she was still sitting on the ground, "I will do anything in my power to help you find true justice. For yourself and your people."

"You believe me?"

Erich thought over the things she had told him. He didn't want to believe them, but sadly they seemed to make more sense than the things he had previously thought. "I do not disbelieve you," he answered eventually. It was the most honest thing he could say at present.

Aizel wanted to march into King Gareth's pristine palace and slap his benevolent young face. Erich's sincerity was the sweetest thing she had ever seen.

"Thank you," she said. "Thank you for listening to me and trusting me."

"Now what?" Erich asked. "I should get you out of here and back to safety. I'm sure I could find a way to get you back to the Isle of . . . I mean, to Istroya." He was looking to the left, his hands counting invisible ideas in the air.

"Erich." She said his name, hoping to draw his attention back to her. "I don't want someone else to save me. I left Istroya because . . ." She paused. She was relieved to finally share critical information with him, but she had already put her sister in danger. ". . . my family is in danger from the taskers, and I need to find a way to get them here. Or, I needed to. Now, I'm not so sure life is safer for them here." She stopped again.

Erich was listening to her, his eyes never leaving her face.

Heartened, Aizel continued, "What I'm trying to say is I don't need you to save me. I just . . . need someone to help me." She could barely whisper the last words. She had never asked for help. "I've never really been in danger from you," she rushed to continue. "This whole thing has been a ruse. King Gareth wants you dead, and if I don't succeed, he'll find another way to do it."

Erich raised his eyebrows. "What? Gareth wants me dead? Are you sure? That seems a little excessive. Isn't he all about justice and uniting the kingdoms and whatnot?"

Aizel rolled her eyes. "He has an interesting way of carrying that out." She dropped the sarcasm from her voice. "Have you lost any of your brothers recently?"

"No," Erich answered. "Well, my older brother did get attacked a few weeks ago. He might be . . . I don't know. I haven't heard from them since we've been traveling."

"That was Gareth. He said your father might miss his sons should something happen to each of them in turn. I'm so sorry." Aizel could imagine what it would be like to lose a beloved sibling.

Erich had gone quite pale. "I need to return to Iseldis and tell my father."

Aizel nodded. "I think that would be best. He may have already targeted another one of your brothers and they need to be warned. Also, would you . . . tell him about us?"

"Us?" Erich looked back up at her quickly.

"Me. The Majis. My people?" Aizel further clarified her question. "Will you tell him what I've told you? Do you think he might . . .?" Her voice wavered. No Quotidian king would ever help them. He might pretend to, but only to further his own gain. The Majis had nothing to offer in return, and no one did favors for free.

Erich had dropped his eyes, looking at the ground as he bit his lower lip. "I can try," he said. "I can try to tell him. It's just that—He hates . . . I don't think he listens to me."

Aizel let that dream fade before it even had a chance to grow roots. "But he'll believe you about Gareth at least?"

"He'll have to. Actually, that part might be easy. He has always been a little wary of Gareth, as was his father King Gael before him. I can convince him to take precautions, although with the coming invasion, he won't want to sever ties completely."

"Why do you think he is targeting your family?" Aizel asked the question that had been stuck in her throat since her first visit to the marble palace.

"I have no idea. We've always been allies." Erich's expression was clouded as he looked back at her. "Wait . . . earlier you said Gareth wants me dead. And if you didn't succeed . . . Have you been plotting . . . Are you going to?"

Aizel shook her head. She glanced up to the darkening sky as she inhaled. She had a voice now. "I was never going to actually do it. But yes, he did send me to . . . kill you."

Erich sat back down on his heels, immediately breaking eye contact with her. His hand fingered the gemstone of the necklace he was still holding. "So, what you're saying is that I was right to fear you all along?" The eyes that turned back to her were filled with distrust.

Aizel shook her head, words failing her—again. "No. Don't turn back on that. The fear I was talking about was a different fear. You were afraid of me because I was . . . different from you. That was the only threat I ever posed to you."

Erich was silent as he processed her words. "Something

still doesn't add up. If you were never going to kill me, why did you even agree to it at all? What were you doing meeting with him and whose side are you on?"

"A few Quotidian soldiers found me on the beach that day after I saved your life, and they brought me all the way here to Chendas. Probably while you were out there looking for me, thinking I was the Majis sorceress."

Erich narrowed his eyes, but the look of anger on his face didn't seem directed at her.

"The king has . . . something that I want." Aizel wanted to trust him with the whole truth.

"Your freedom?" Erich's face remained clouded and confused.

"Something like that." Aizel still had to save Celesta. She was returning to the marble palace no matter what, and she wasn't going to let Erich come along and get himself killed. If he knew the full truth, he would never let her go back alone. He was too good for that. "He threatened my family if I don't come back with proof of your death."

"You're going back?"

Aizel nodded.

"Let me come with you." His confusion made way for sincerity.

Aizel smiled, both at his earnestness and her foreseeing exactly what he would do. "No. He wants you dead. You should go back to Iseldis and warn your family. Keep your brothers safe."

"But what about you?"

"As long as I can prove you are dead, my family will be fine." She chose her words carefully without fully answering his question. It didn't matter what happened to her as long as Celesta was safe.

Erich nodded. "Proof that I am dead? I think we can manage that."

CHAPTER 34

*E*rich held the reins of both horses, trying not to stare at the brilliant flashes of red the sun illuminated in Aizel's hair. He was failing miserably.

"I don't have anywhere safe to keep Constance," Aizel said, patting the mare on the nose in farewell. "You weren't so bad after all."

Erich felt a flutter of pride in his chest until he realized her last words were directed at the horse and not him.

"Stay out of sight and be safe." This time, she wasn't talking to the horse.

"You too," Erich replied. "I mean, stay safe. And stay out of sight if you can."

She smiled at him. It was a nice but guarded smile. "Goodbye, Captain Erich of the Iseldis elite guard."

Erich wasn't ready to say goodbye. The short, quiet girl in front of him had only just found her voice, and he was sure she had more interesting things to say. He wasn't ready to let her go. He attempted a smile of his own, but it probably looked more fake than hers.

She shifted her weight from one foot to the next, waiting for him to say goodbye so she could leave.

"If you ever need anything, you know where to find me," he offered, wondering if he would ever see her again.

She nodded. "In Iseldis, in the capital."

"I live in the big palace up the hill overlooking the city. It's hard to miss. Shouldn't be a problem finding it. You should come there as soon as you are done. I can help you help your family. Especially if they are in danger. I'm sure we can find a way to keep them safe in Iseldis." He stopped speaking only when he'd run out of words to beg her with.

"I thought you said your father wasn't ready to accept the Majis?"

"I'll try to talk to him. But I don't need his aid. I can find a way to help you. Just . . . please let me know you made it safely away from King Gareth." He looked at her with all the care he dared to show.

"I'll find a way to get word to you," she said. "Now go make sure your family is safe. That's the most important thing."

He nodded. She was right.

"Goodbye, Erich."

"Goodbye, Azel."

The glare she sent him was worth it.

He couldn't help the grin that spread over his face as she turned her back and walked toward the main road.

"Aizel." He whispered her name to himself. One single person—who had been unable to speak for most of their time together—had opened up his entire world.

He wanted to run after her, to make sure she was safe in a city full of fearful quotidian people. It wasn't as though Gareth would make an attempt on his life in the middle of such a crowded city. But if he did, there would be no one left to warn Erich's family.

And, as Aizel had said, making sure they were safe was the most important thing. But as her shimmering red hair finally faded from view, he couldn't help but question whether that was true. Yes, of course, he wanted his family to be safe and to figure out what was going on—but he had never spent an entire month with someone and still felt as though he could never fully get to know everything about them.

Even if he never saw her again, he would never forget her.

Not that he had any hope of ever pursuing a romantic relationship with her. He had been completely horrible to her. For days.

For a single moment, he allowed himself the luxury of imagining his life with her in it. He would make sure she never wanted for anything ever again, and he would make sure she was safe from any quotidian fool who dared to laugh at her.

She would laugh with him when he made a good jest, and she would hold him accountable when his ideas were incorrect. He would be an ever-changing person if she were in his life to challenge him. And that was the furthest thing from boring he could imagine.

The fantasy was perfect.

Red hair, green eyes, and crossed arms would probably haunt his dreams forever.

Dreams.

He hadn't had a nightmare since that second night she'd woken him up. He'd gotten so distracted spending time with her and thinking about her that he hadn't even been afraid of water.

"Thank you, Aizel," he whispered to the empty forest.

With a final sigh, he turned to the two horses. This was about so much more than his own happiness. It was about the fate of the entire continent. He had to get back to his father.

The skin on his arm tingled in discomfort as he imagined facing his father and convincing him that the evil Majis were not the villains. Especially after he'd heard his father's whispered anger the night Aden had been attacked.

Erich had no proof to back up his claims, only the word of a Majis. If his father could only meet Aizel, he would see how trustworthy she was. It would be so much easier if he could bring Aizel back with him.

He closed his eyes, wishing the wishful thinking away.

Since he was supposed to be dead, he slipped into his guard uniform so as not to draw attention to himself. The gray would make him blend in like any other guard.

Then he mounted his horse and began to make his way down the road, away from Chendas.

The forest was too dense to travel through with both horses, but it would clear up higher in the mountains. He would be able to travel more quickly and spend the majority of the trip in secrecy.

Or at least he would have been able to—if a small contingent of soldiers led by General Gautho himself hadn't appeared on the road a few hours later.

Erich glanced around him, but it was too late. The general had seen him.

"Captain!" Gautho called out. "I'm glad to have caught you!"

Erich reined in his horse and waited for the general to approach. Perhaps this wasn't such a bad thing. If the war against the Majis were fabricated, the general would need to know.

Gautho rode up to Erich. The general's men trotted around him, stopping just past Erich.

"General," Erich greeted him. "How are things going on the coast?"

"The attacks have increased again," Gautho responded. "I came to speak with King Gareth in person to make a report and request additional aid."

"That may not be wise," Erich said, picking his words with care. "I have some news to discuss with you first."

The general narrowed his eyes. "You are alone? I take it you have delivered the sorceress?"

"About that . . ." Erich glanced at the Chendas soldiers on either side of him. "Perhaps we could speak in private?"

"You took off that girl's necklace." Gautho's lips curled into a sneer.

"What?" Erich's voice came out with an uncontrollable squeak.

"Turio was right. You fell for her wiles and let her go free."

The soldiers around him moved closer, hemming him in.

"No!" Erich cried. "You have to listen to me! We've got this war all wrong."

"Oh, do we?" Gautho jerked his head toward one of his men.

"The Majis are not launching this attack," Erich cried in a rush. "It's someone else, and I think that someone is—"

Pain exploded in the back of his head.

Then everything went black.

CHAPTER 35

Aizel arrived at the gates of the marble palace during the middle of the day. Given the secrecy King Gareth and Turio had enforced, she had a feeling it would irk them for her to show up in broad daylight.

To her delight, it did. She was quickly waved inside, shown to a small room, and instructed to wait until the king was ready to see her.

Of course, he wasn't ready to see her until many hours after the sun had fallen—another nod to secrecy.

Standing outside the column-like room where she had met him previously, Aizel waited as one of the guards removed the white ribbon from around her neck. Erich had replaced the spelled gem on the white ribbon with a shiny rock from the bottom of the riverbed.

Entering the room, Aizel noticed once again how the ceiling above her was so high the flickering light of the torches couldn't even reach it. It made her feel as though she were looking up into an endless hole. Perhaps it would feel more welcoming during the daylight, but she didn't particularly care to find out.

Standing before the king, she waited for him to initiate the conversation. As before, he was flanked by two older men, and two hooded figures stood at the back of the room behind her.

The king merely sat on the front edge of his tall, thin throne, staring at her intently as he ignored the whispering of the advisors beside him.

Two could play at that game.

Aizel stared back at him, unafraid to look directly into his eyes.

After several long moments, even his advisors stopped whispering. Young or not, this man could command a room.

Finally, King Gareth raised his eyebrows.

Taking that as her cue to report, Aizel reached inside her sack and removed a long, colorful feather. The vanes were crumpled, and the shaft was bent in multiple places.

"I bring you justice," Aizel said, her clear voice ringing off the bare stone walls and echoing up into the cavernous ceiling. The tip of the feather in her hand dropped toward the floor, a crusted substance at its end weighing it down.

"The body?" The king reached out his hand.

Before Aizel could step forward, a guard appeared at her side and took the feather from her. Bringing it to the base of the throne, he handed it to the king.

The sight of the sad feather swinging precariously at its broken joints caused Aizel's whole body to tense. She barely stopped her hands from tightening into fists. For her, that same plume had become synonymous with its owner. It was happy and carefree and a little excessive. Just like Erich was talkative, colorful, and animated.

Seeing the broken feather in the king's hand—as opposed to swaying freely above Erich's head—made her chest squeeze tight in fear. She had considered killing him in the beginning. And he wasn't out of danger. When the king found out he was alive . . .

Suddenly, she desperately wanted Erich to live. Not that she cared for him . . .

She did care for him. And not despite his self-absorbed ramblings and unfiltered comments, but because of them. She had never known someone who could sustain such constant lightheartedness or who had no fear of speaking honestly.

Everyone on Istroya—all the Majis, that was—were exhausted. Yes, they were joyful and occasionally even happy, but that was a rare gift. And none of them had the luxury of honesty. Her mother would always warn her never to speak of the secrets they whispered at night—secrets of magic and freedom and times long gone.

The thought of the real Erich being as broken and dead as the crumpled feather overwhelmed her with grief.

He's not actually dead, she reminded herself. *He's alive and well and even believed me.*

The king was staring at her expectantly. He had asked her a question.

Her mind raced, asking her ears if they had heard the words and remembered them. "Where is his body?" she finally stuttered. It was fine; she'd been prepared for that question. She took a big breath, stabilizing herself to refocus on the task at hand. "His body is in a large meadow west of the city walls. I . . . it's over the edge of a cliff and may be difficult to access. I didn't know what else to do with it to keep it a secret and all."

"And you feel satisfied you have repaid what you stole from me?" The king swooshed the feather in front of his knees.

Aizel nodded, glancing to the side as she considered his question. She hadn't planned an answer for this one since she hadn't expected him to ask it. He was going to be the judge of the equitability of their deal, and they both knew it. He was the Quotidian king. He would do what he wanted regardless of her opinion on the matter.

Rather than lie by answering his question, Aizel decided to push her own interests. "I have done as you asked. I have given you his life. You promised me a life in return. Where is my sister?"

The king sighed as he leaned back in his chair. "You disappoint me, sorceress."

Aizel felt an odd tingling sensation run down her arm and over the back of her hand. She shifted uncomfortably, resisting the urge to rush forward and attack the smug young man sitting on the throne. Something was wrong.

"It is my greatest desire to unite the Five Kingdoms under a single banner, a unified whole." His eyes were wide with concern. And hurt. "I thought we agreed on this point. I thought you would help me to achieve this dream. But no, you are like so many others, willing to put yourself before the good of the whole. Turio was right."

Aizel shook her head, taking a step back from the sincere-looking young man. In some ways, he reminded her of Erich—but a version of Erich who was entirely too selfish to learn and grow.

That was another thing she loved about Erich. He had grown and changed each time he'd been presented with a new truth.

She pushed that thought aside. For now, she had to focus and save her sister. She hoped the king wasn't toying with her, that he had not already harmed Celesta.

"What do you mean, Your Majesty?" she asked, using every possible ounce of her willpower to keep her voice at its proper pitch. "We made a deal, and I kept up my end of the bargain."

"Did you?" His voice was slightly higher than it had been. He lifted his hand toward a door on the opposite side of the room. "Because when I make a bargain, I keep it."

Aizel's heart dropped before the door even opened. Something was definitely wrong. She hoped against hope that Celesta would walk into the room as a guard opened the door.

The only other person it could be was Erich.

But there was no way the king had already discovered Erich was still alive. He was in hiding, making his way back to Iseldis. If the king had found him, he would be dead or in chains.

A familiar figure entered.

And it wasn't her sister.

Prince Erich strode into the room. His dark gray uniform held his shoulders in a stiff position. His eyes were dark, and his mouth was pinched. He quickly scanned the room, lifting his eyebrows when he saw her. He looked exactly like the same spoiled, distant, coldhearted boy who had scoffed at her in the underground cellar by the sea.

He hadn't changed at all.

Anger erupted inside her. He had been toying with her all along.

Of course he had.

He was one of them. He was literally wearing the uniform

of a Quotidian soldier. Why had she ever allowed herself to trust?

From the corner of her eye, she saw two guards approaching. One was holding out a white ribbon. The gem was bright green—not the gray riverbed rock.

Aizel kept her gaze on the front of the room. *"Traitor!"* She screamed the word in her mind, hoping it came out in the angry glare of her eyes. He was no longer worth her concern. She had no time to fight him.

"Where is Celesta?!" Aizel yelled.

"Gareth, what is going on?" Erich asked at the same time.

The two guards were standing at her side now.

Inhaling a deep breath, Aizel briefly heard her words colliding with Erich's on the stone walls, reverberating through the room in a dissonant jumble of sound.

Opening her mouth, she shouted out the first notes that came to her mind. They were discordant and minor, building on the echoes of sound that were climbing higher up the cavernous ceiling.

King Gareth clutched the armrests of his throne, his eyes going wide. The advisors beside his throne leapt back against the wall, putting as much distance as they could between her and themselves.

Erich whipped his head from Gareth to face her, awe and fear in his eyes.

Be afraid, traitor, she thought, increasing the volume of her voice so that she was practically yelling.

Then the pain hit her.

It felt as though someone had stabbed her in the back. But rather than concentrated pain in one area, it spread throughout her entire body, intensifying as it went.

Her breath left her body. She couldn't even scream.

She fell to the floor as her legs collapsed under her.

The two hooded figures who had been standing at the back of the room had stepped forward, their hands outstretched and their long, pale fingers twisted and bent as though they were grabbing the air itself.

Aizel had seen this happen before, although she had been fortunate enough to never have felt it.

It was Quotidian magic. The taskers used it when a Majis showed any sign of using their magic outside of their approved work.

She couldn't move. She couldn't breathe.

The last thing she saw before squeezing her eyes shut against the pain were dirty fingernails. They belonged to the Quotidian mage who used his outstretched hand to fuel his cruel magic with her own pain.

She tried to inhale, stopping her mind from panicking. If she could create any kind of harmony within herself, she could break the flow of their magic.

But it was too much. She sagged against the floor.

"Munney?" Erich's voice sounded surprised, but she was too engrossed in her own pain to decipher what the strange word meant.

Finally, it stopped.

It took several moments for her lungs to finally open and accept new air.

She focused on her breath for a while, her body exhausted.

When she regained the strength to lift her head, Erich was no longer in the room.

"Where is my sister?" Aizel yelled, but no sound left her mouth. She dropped her head in defeat, the familiar weight of a single jewel bobbing against her neck.

CHAPTER 36

*E*rich was sure he was about to die. Every time he heard a sound outside the door, he tensed. King Gareth wanted him dead, and it seemed that Gautho was in on it, too.

When footsteps stopped just outside, Erich moved to the center of the room. He would not be taken by surprise.

"Erich, my young friend, what a pleasant surprise to see you." King Gareth held out his hand as he entered the small windowless space.

"I thought you were expecting me with . . . the Majis sorceress." Erich could not say her name in front of Gareth. It felt too personal, like he was sharing a secret that didn't belong to him.

"But that's not what happened, now, is it?" Gareth smiled, his face open and honest despite the menacing threat behind his words.

Erich had been waiting in this small room for hours. It

was richly furnished, but the single doorway had been heavily guarded, and he hadn't been allowed to leave.

"Would you care to enlighten me as to why you failed in your duty?" Gareth asked.

"I don't think my duty was ever your intent, was it?"

Gareth looked taken aback. "I'm not at all sure what you mean, my dear brother. General Gautho said you were given clear orders. Yet, the woman you were supposed to escort showed up on my doorstep—alone—claiming to have killed you."

Erich said nothing as he waited for Gareth to get to his point.

"I was quite devastated to hear of your death," Gareth finally continued. "I've always admired you. You are different from your father and brothers—in a good way." He hurried to correct himself. "You have a spark that they do not. You see things differently than they do."

Erich watched and listened as Gareth paced the room. Honestly, the king was quite right in his assessments thus far. Not that it meant anything.

"What you need is a chance to prove yourself. Under the right . . . mentor . . . I think you could become something far greater than the fourth in line to the throne of Iseldis." Gareth stopped pacing, cutting his eyes at Erich as if to gauge his reaction.

"Who would you suggest as the right mentor?" A plan was forming in Erich's head. If he could convince Gareth to let him live, he might be able to find and save Aizel.

"Myself," Gareth answered, another smile gracing his features.

Erich raised his eyebrows, pretending to be interested in

what the king was saying. "What are you offering to teach me?"

"Teach you? No. That sounds so juvenile. You're a man now, Erich, not a child. Share. I have things I could share with you." Gareth's open face was so hopeful Erich almost laughed out loud.

For a moment, he wondered if this was how young ladies felt when men they despised tried to woo them. "What things could you share with me?" he asked, hoping to glean any information he could.

Gareth's eyes fell. "My burdens, for one." He looked to the left. "I've been given a very heavy responsibility in this life. I was barely your age when my father died, and I was forced to follow in his great footsteps with no brother to help me carry the weight."

"What weight?" Erich asked, hoping his interest would keep the king talking.

"My father should have been the one to defend our kingdoms against the Majis. He was a true leader, one who could unite people and carry out the kind of plans no one else could even conceive of." Gareth sighed. "I am doing my best, but there is so much I cannot see."

"How can I help you carry the weight, my king?"

Gareth looked up. The hope in his eyes made him appear even younger than he was. "You have such a keen knowledge of battle. If you could focus on the Majis, I could devote my attention to uniting the kingdoms."

Erich nodded, as though considering the king's offer. "Are not the Five Kingdoms already united?"

Gareth took a moment before answering. "There are . . . some complications that make it more difficult than it appears."

"And what about General Gautho? Is he not the most skilled and knowledgeable for this task?"

Erich's main goal was to get out of this situation with his life, and he would continue to ask any question that came to mind.

"General Gautho will command the front line, of course. He is certainly the most competent in that area. But you've seen how stretched thin he is. He cannot be both here with me and on the coast. You could fulfill one of those roles, taking a weight off the good general and myself."

"But why me?"

"Do you want this or not?" For a moment, Gareth seemed to lose his patience.

"Of course, I want it badly!" Erich said quickly to placate the king. "It is an opportunity my father would never have given me. I'm just . . . I'm humbled by your trust, my lord."

Gareth smiled. "Then it is settled. Come."

For now, Erich thought. *At least until I can find out where they've taken Aizel and get us both out of here.*

CHAPTER 37

As the iron grate of the dungeon clanged shut behind her, Aizel heard a new finality in the ugly sound.

This time she really was stuck.

She had assumed she'd eventually end up here, but only after Celesta was free. She hadn't even managed to accomplish that.

Then there was Erich, with his cold, distant face as he'd stormed into the room. He was a Quotidian soldier—what had she expected? That he would actually do something for someone else's gain?

She sank to the floor of the small, dim cell. The rough stone was cold and wet, but she didn't even register the water as it soaked through her thin dress.

She had failed.

It was over.

Celesta was gone, forever.

Her stomach turned as she thought about what would happen to her younger sister. She leaned over as her body attempted to heave the contents of her empty stomach, almost happy for the physical pain to distract her from her thoughts.

"Are you alright?" a raspy voice asked from her left.

"*No,*" she answered honestly, but no sound came out. She shook her head, not even caring to look up and find the source of the voice. It sounded like an old man. A weak old man.

"I guess that is a rather stupid question to ask someone in a dungeon cell." He chuckled at his own humor, but the laugh turned into a dry, racking cough.

The cough lasted for what felt like an eternity. Aizel listened in alarm, afraid the ancient one would expire before he was able to draw another breath.

Finally, the painful sound ceased and was replaced by a slow wheeze.

As her eyes adjusted to the dim light, she saw the old man in the cell next to hers. Only an iron grill separated them.

He sat with his back to the one stone wall of his cell. His hand clutched one of the iron bars between them as though using it to steady himself through the coughs.

"*Are you alright?*" she tried to whisper, forgetting her own woes for a moment. His face was pale and thin, but it was mostly covered by a soft white beard.

"This humidity in the air has gotten to me," he said when he finally caught his breath. His earlier humor had disappeared.

Aizel breathed in, feeling the cold air inside her. It wasn't a pleasant feeling.

When she didn't respond, he turned to look at her. His eyes were a soft brown, hidden under bushy white eyebrows.

They were kind to look at, but she dropped her gaze. She wasn't quite ready to make another friend.

"You're a Majis."

She instinctively shrank away from him, glad their cells were separate.

"And they've muted you." His voice was kind as well. "If you would like, I can remove the necklace for you."

Aizel glanced up at him. The expression on his face told her he was serious.

Part of her wanted to curl up on the wet, cold stone floor and cry herself to sleep. What would it matter if she never opened her mouth again?

But he was offering, and she had nothing to lose.

She scooted her back toward the grill between them and flipped her voluminous hair around her shoulder.

A moment later, she felt the ties around her neck loosen as the necklace slipped away.

She exhaled in relief. The weight was gone.

Turning back to face the old man, she smiled. "Thank you."

He held the necklace out to her through the bars.

She took it from him. She could at least pretend to wear it whenever someone came down for her—if someone ever would.

"How long have you been here?" she asked, hoping to keep the fear from her voice.

"Six seasons. Eight," he replied. "I can't remember."

Aizel felt a scratchy sensation at the back of her throat as she breathed in the thick air. Her lungs seemed to seize up. Would she be rasping and coughing in six seasons? Or would it be sooner?

The thought of spending more than a few days in the

dank, dark cell made her lungs seize up again, and she struggled to breathe.

"Why did they put you in here?" For all she knew, he could be a murderer, but she could use the distraction. Besides, from what she had witnessed of the king's justice, this man was likely anything but.

"I helped Majis escape from Istroya," he answered. "My ship was intercepted on my last journey, and I was arrested for treason. I don't regret it." He said the last words with force, and Aizel heard a spark of the man he had once been.

If he was arrested six or eight seasons ago, that would mean . . .

"Peter," she breathed. "You're Peter."

He glanced away. "It's been a long time since I've heard my name."

"You didn't show up to the meeting place for your last delivery, so we assumed you were dead. Or worse." Aizel looked at the gaunt man sitting across from her. "I guess it was worse."

"I'm so sorry I didn't arrive in time. I have worried ever since about the ones I was supposed to get out."

Aizel's heart broke at his kindness. He had been rotting in a dungeon cell for years, and he was apologizing to her. "Thank you. I heard that you were once a rich nobleman in your old life. You sacrificed much to work against the horrible injustices of King Gareth."

"I'm not a hero, girl. Just a man who couldn't bear to sit in comfort while others were suffering. I did what every man and woman should."

Again, Aizel was completely humbled. And baffled. "But you didn't even know us. You aren't one of us."

"But I knew you had been immeasurably wronged. And I

had the position and means to do something about it. It was my privilege to put them at the service of your people."

The selflessness of his words soothed Aizel in a way that nothing else had. Perhaps she wasn't as alone as she had always assumed.

"Thank you," she whispered. "I wish I could save you in return." She meant her words, but the stark reality of their situation crashed into every crack of her emotions.

"My dear girl." The old man peered at her through the iron bars with smiling eyes. "You have a voice. Use it."

*A*izel's eyes opened wide as she stared at Peter's smiling face.

Perhaps she was going crazy from the stress and exhaustion of the day, but she felt a small tremor rising in her core. It grew and bubbled and expanded until it rippled out in a small giggle. The giggle grew into laughter, and she hugged her knees as tears formed in her eyes.

"I do have a voice, don't I?" she said. "I'm afraid I'd entirely forgotten it existed. 'Be quiet, Aizel, don't speak. The taskers might hear you.'" She mimicked the words her parents had constantly repeated.

She kept her laughter quiet, not knowing who might be listening. But the rough-hewn stone walls quickly swallowed the sound.

With a deep exhale, she turned her attention back to Peter.

His shoulders shook as he laughed along with her.

"Can you say that again?" she asked.

He looked confused for a moment, then flicked his snowy eyebrows. "You have a voice, my dear. A powerful, harmonizing voice that can change this world. Use it."

Aizel straightened her shoulders, basking in the affirmation of his words. "That is the sweetest music I have ever heard."

"I'll repeat it as often as you'd like."

"I might take you up on that," Aizel replied. "But for now, let us find a way to get out of here."

"Now that is the sweetest music I have ever heard." Peter pulled himself up to a standing position, still holding the iron bars for support.

Aizel glanced at the area around her. They were in a tiny underground dungeon. She couldn't fully see into the other two cells, but they appeared empty.

"Where are the other prisoners? Surely King Gareth has more than just you and I?"

"This is for magical prisoners only. He doesn't want us spreading our 'lies' to other lawbreakers. Could you imagine how that would work out for him? No, this section is only for those who know too much. Also . . ." He lowered his voice until it was barely audible. "It's closer to the examiners' wing."

Aizel looked over at the old man. She had no idea who the examiners were, but from the clouded look on Peter's face, she didn't want to know.

"Good. That should make this easier then. Except . . ." If this was the prison for the Majis, where was Celesta? "Did you happen to have any visitors in the last few weeks? Maybe another Majis? A young girl?"

"Aw, yes." He lifted his hands above his head and wiggled his fingers as he swept them in a wide downward arc.

Aizel's heart warmed upon recognizing the symbol for her sister's name. "Celesta," she whispered.

"Celesta?" Peter tilted his head. "Like the stars. That suits her."

"You learned to speak with her?" Aizel asked in disbelief.

"Of course. We had many fine conversations. She cheered me."

Aizel smiled, relieved and heartened that her sister hadn't been alone. "Do you know where she is now?"

"No. They came for her this morning."

His words sank in her stomach, but Aizel forced herself to stay focused on the task at hand.

She listened to the space around her. It was absolutely silent, but in a tangibly thick way, like the seashore on a foggy morning.

The lack of sound was oppressive. It made her feel even more cold and uncomfortable. She wouldn't be able to draw on the harmony around her. She would have to channel her magic by bringing the harmony from within herself.

She closed her eyes. Her stomach twisted with thoughts of Celesta. Her ankle was stiff, still not fully healed. Her muscles felt weak and tired after the attack of the Quotidian mages. She didn't feel peace.

Her heart started to race. If she couldn't find a way to channel harmony, she would have nothing with which to power her magic.

When she had needed to use magic as a diver, she'd always had the peaceful presence of the ocean to give her strength, or the augmented use of the lotus-scented oil— which was still in the small sack hanging from her side!

But it was poisoned.

Pulling the bottle from her bag, she dropped to her knees

and looked for a crack in the stone floor. Unstopping the vial, she carefully poured its contents into it. She would never use such a thing on another living person.

The lotus scent filled the small space, but it carried a sickly-sweet smell that was unusual.

Aizel put the vial back in her sack and stood away from the area.

Peter watched her movements, but he didn't question her.

She stopped, looking back at the old man. He was calm. He had been here for a long time, but he had remained self-less and humble. He was close to being peaceful despite his unfortunate circumstances.

Aizel nodded. Just thinking of his actions relaxed her chest. She could work with that. She was thankful he had risked everything to try and get her sister—and others—to safety.

She smiled at him, thanking him in silence, then turned to examine the grated door. It was made of interconnected iron rods. Reaching through, she could feel the large lock connected to the door handle.

She shook it, testing its strength.

The lock wouldn't come off easily.

Perhaps she could force the iron bars into a hole large enough for them to step through?

She stood back. Her toes tingled, and her fingers felt rest-less. She was excited to use her voice but incredibly nervous. Throughout her life, she'd rarely had the chance to use it in an experimental capacity.

Yes, she could use magic to change the world around her, but she barely knew how.

Music was the best way to channel harmony, and it was

easy to use song to manipulate the emotions of people around her.

Manipulating matter was far more difficult.

Closing her eyes, she began to hum. She started with a melody she knew well, but the notes came out flat.

Inhaling, she started over. She imagined the iron bars moving slowly out of the way, bending their shape to let her pass through them. Slowly, she gained confidence and started to sing the words to the song. They were in the ancient language her mother had always sung in. She didn't know the words, but they sounded beautiful.

She was tempted to open her eyes after the first verse, but she knew she would lose momentum if the magic hadn't started working. So, she finished all four of the verses she knew.

Then she cracked open a single eye.

The metal bars remained firmly in place.

She opened both eyes, her shoulders slumping in defeat.

"That was beautiful," Peter said. "My lungs are breathing easier than they have in a long time."

"Thanks," Aizel muttered. "But it did us no good."

"It did me some good."

"It needs to do more good," Aizel countered. She stepped forward to the grated door, shaking it on its hinges without making a sound. Maybe she was trying to exert too large a change in the world around her. Perhaps she should focus on the hinges only?

The heavy lock clanked against the door.

Or maybe she should focus on the lock? That was an idea.

Reaching through the doorway, she touched the lock with her fingers. She couldn't see it, but she could feel its large keyhole. It was big enough to almost slip her smallest finger inside.

Closing her eyes again, she began to sing the same song. This time, she imagined the tines of the lock turning back into place so they aligned. They wanted to be aligned; it was their proper form.

She sang the first verse, focusing on the beauty of the melody and the familiar lilt of the unfamiliar words.

A small clank distracted her for a moment, and her skin tingled.

She continued to sing, afraid she had imagined it.

During the third verse, a much louder clanging came from Peter's cell, and she opened her eyes.

Peter was standing in the central area of the dungeon. The door to his cell hung wide open.

He grinned at her.

Jumping forward, Aizel reached around her own door and pulled against the lock. It opened with a click, and she leaned her shoulder into the heavy door.

It swung open with a rusty squeak.

She felt light and unstoppable. Another giggle formed in her throat. She did have a powerful voice.

CHAPTER 39

"Your first task as my new commander is quite simple," Gareth said, leading Erich through the windowless halls of the marble castle.

Erich had always admired the monolithic architecture of the tall, white palace. But tonight he felt as though the tall walls kept moving closer and closer together. His heart raced as they reminded him of being stuck underwater. How had he never noticed this castle had no windows?

"It will take place as soon as the sun rises. I've already sent notices out all over the city, so we should have good attendance."

Erich ignored his rapidly beating heart and gave his attention back to the king. Hopefully, he could catch up on what Gareth was telling him.

"You always have to keep the peasants entertained," Gareth continued. "But you know that." The king stopped walking and turned to Erich, placing a hand on his shoulder. "You know what it's like to grow up as the son of a king.

Your whole life has been sacrificed for the good of your people. Very few men understand what that's like. I appreciate that we share this."

Erich tried not to flinch away from Gareth's forced sincerity. If he didn't know any better, he would be completely captivated by the young king's words.

He had known Gareth his whole life and Aizel for only a handful of days. Yet, he trusted Aizel infinitely more.

"We are different, you and I." Erich's lips quirked at the duplicitousness of his own words. Ian would have been proud of his diplomacy. Hopefully, the king would think Erich was agreeing with him that they were unique and special. What Erich was actually saying was that they were different from each other.

"Can you handle that?" Gareth continued down the hallway.

"I think so," Erich responded, still unsure what he was agreeing to. He should have paid more attention to that part of the conversation. "Could you explain exactly what steps I'll need to take? I don't want to make a mistake from the very beginning." He so wished Ian were present to witness his cleverness.

"I have no doubt you'll do a splendid job. All you have to do is read the notice to spectators and oversee the execution to make sure the Majis sorceress doesn't escape."

Erich's feet froze. His first task was to execute Aizel?

Gareth hadn't seemed to notice Erich's reaction as the king himself stopped, waiting for two guards to open the door at the end of the hall.

"I think it will give the message everyone needs to hear right now," Gareth said. "It's all about balancing the right amount of fear with the right amount of trust. We want them to be afraid of the Majis but to trust us implicitly, you see."

"Even though the Majis don't pose a threat?" Erich couldn't keep playing this game. Not when the game risked innocent lives.

"Exactly." Gareth's voice had lost some of its syrupy quality, and Erich guessed the king might no longer be putting on a show. "I knew you would see things differently than your father."

Erich followed Gareth through the open doorway and into the room where he had last seen Aizel.

"My lord, I do not think I . . ." Erich stopped himself. He wanted to make it out of this alive, but more than that, he wanted Aizel to survive as well. Perhaps, if he bit his tongue, he could pretend to oversee this execution but still save her. "I don't think that should be a problem," he finished with confidence.

"Excellent." Gareth grinned as he sat down on the only chair in the small room.

Erich thought it a little excessive he had a special throne even in his personal meeting room.

"Your Majesty!" A guard ran into the room, bowing low before his king.

Gareth sat up. Concern was written all over his face. "What is it?"

"She's gone!" the guard said.

Erich's chest swelled with hope.

Gareth's face darkened. "Who is gone?"

"The Majis sorceress. She took Peter with her." The guard was still bent over, and Erich could feel the fear radiating off him. "She left this." He held up a white ribbon weighted down with a gem.

Gareth relaxed back on his throne and waved his hand in dismissal. "That's not an issue. We can execute the younger one instead. She's still here, right?"

"Yes! Yes, Your Majesty. It was wise of you to remove her from the west dungeon."

"Bring her in," Gareth said. "Keep her here until the execution so there are no other possible mishaps."

"Yes, Your Majesty." The guard stood, relief covering his face. "I've sent out a search party, Your Majesty. We should have the older one located as soon as possible."

Gareth waved dismissively again. "She's an untrained Majis. There's not much she can do. Bring her to me when you find her."

The guard bowed once more and left the room.

Erich pinched his lips closed to keep the grin from his face. All he had to do now was escape and locate Aizel.

CHAPTER 40

Getting out of the palace in the dead of night was surprisingly easy.

"You seem to know this place quite well for having been stuck in its dungeon," Aizel whispered as they slipped through a dark, empty corridor.

"I was a frequent visitor here in another life," Peter replied. "The only thing I don't know is where the back entrances are. Those should be easier to leave through undetected, I would think."

"This feels more like the servant's quarters than anything else," Aizel responded.

"I smell yeast." Peter lifted his nose. "I think the kitchens might be this way."

Aizel followed him down another twist in the hallway. Sure enough, it opened into an enormous kitchen.

Peter held her back in the shadows of the hall. "I can see at least two scullery maids still working."

"At this hour?" Aizel was surprised.

"The kitchen never sleeps." Peter turned back to her. His face was shadowed, but she could hear the smile in his voice. "Unless a Majis melody makes them drowsy?"

"That it does." Closing her eyes, Aizel slowly hummed the sleeping song. It was so quiet, she could barely hear it herself.

She wanted the magic to work its effects before she had to sing louder and alert the kitchen staff of their presence.

She sent the melody into the kitchen, filling her voice with as much soothing sleepiness as she could.

Peter touched her arm. "I think you've done it."

She opened her eyes.

He was already stepping into the large room. Sticking to the shadowed areas, they quickly made their way past the two girls. One was leaning over the counter, her hands—and now face—buried in flour. The other had fallen asleep standing against the wall with a broom in her hand.

Aizel hoped they woke peacefully before their taskers found they had nodded off.

The kitchen opened to a large ungated courtyard. Moments later, she and Peter were speeding down the open road.

He was breathing heavily, so she wrapped her arm through his. "We did it," she whispered, hoping to hearten the old man. "Let's put as much distance between us and that marble monstrosity as we can."

Peter nodded, not bothering to waste his precious breath on speaking.

Aizel had no idea where they were going, but they turned onto the nearest side street and walked quietly in the shadows of the nearby homes and fences.

She helped Peter move along as quickly as she could. She

didn't want to rush the old man, but she was also anxious to get as far away as possible.

"Here." Peter pointed down the back of a rundown alleyway.

"You know this area?" Aizel couldn't see much in the darkness, but this particular street was definitely leading them away from the finer homes in the city. That felt like a good thing.

Peter nodded. "I have friends close by."

Aizel moved forward with a renewed energy of her own. They had been walking for less than an hour when Peter finally indicated a wooden building up ahead. Its metal sign hung from a post. Three large letters spelled out "Ale." A metal bird with large, sharp claws sat atop the sign.

Aizel wasn't particularly fond of taverns, but she trusted Peter's friends more than she did Erich's.

"Back door," Peter wheezed.

She led them around the building where they finally stopped, catching their breaths in the darkness.

"You're sure this is safe?" she asked. "Even . . . for me?"

"It was safe two years ago," Peter responded. "I can't promise more than that." Reaching out, he tapped on the door, knocking out a specific rhythm on the wooden surface.

Aizel glanced around the alley. She hoped it was loud enough to wake the owners of the establishment but quiet enough not to wake anyone else.

Finally, she heard footsteps on the other side of the door.

Peter pulled back his hand and stepped protectively in front of her.

Appreciating the gesture—even though he was in a far worse condition than she was—Aizel placed her hand on his shoulder.

The door creaked open quietly, and a woman's face peered out. She was wearing a fluffy nightcap and had a blanket wrapped around her shoulders. "What is the most powerful weapon?" she whispered.

Aizel couldn't make out her face in the darkness, but she imagined the woman was squinting at them.

"Harmony," Peter whispered back.

The lady stepped back into the house, pushing the door open for them to enter.

When they were safely inside with the door closed, she lit a small lantern.

When she could finally see them properly, the woman's face went as white as the nightcap on her head. "Peter? Is that really you?"

"Aye, Doona, it is."

"We thought you were dead. All this time."

Aizel could see tears forming in the woman's eyes. She stepped forward and wrapped her arms around him.

"It's good to see you, my friend," Doona said as she clung to him. She blinked her eyes rapidly, then noticed Aizel standing behind Peter. "Oh dearie, you look a right sight! Come in and get warm and I'll find you some food."

Doona swiveled on her heel and stirred the buried coals in the large fireplace behind her. She waved Aizel closer and then disappeared through an open doorway.

Peter sat in a wooden chair. He looked exhausted.

Aizel knelt in front of the coals, softly blowing on them to encourage their flames.

"She seems quite unbothered by this," Aizel said.

"Mmh?" Peter responded.

"Is she used to taking in hungry runaways off the streets?"

Aizel dropped her voice to a whisper as the woman returned, carrying a plate with bread and cheese.

"It's what Mama Doona does best," Peter responded, keeping his voice low as well.

"What was that?" Doona handed the plate to Aizel.

"I was saying that your bread is the best in town." Peter smiled as he reached for a roll.

Doona beamed. "That surely hasn't changed. Eat that slowly, though, so you don't upset your stomach. Would you like some tea, dearie?"

Realizing the woman was talking to her, Aizel tilted her head up. She swallowed the bite of bread in her mouth with a squeak. "Yes, please."

Mama Doona patted her on the head like she was still a child and bustled back to a cupboard near the door.

Aizel felt the soft heat of the fire melting away her stress.

"How are the others?" Peter turned toward their host.

Others? Suddenly, it hit Aizel. The bird on the sign out front, the secret password to get in—this was the River's Talon! Or at least it was their meeting place. Hope spread over her. If anyone could help her get Celesta back from Gareth, it was this group of brave heroes—and they were unquestionably heroes, regardless of what Peter thought of himself.

"Luck is finally on your side tonight. Robin is actually here. Right now. Haven't seen her in a month but then she shows up the same night you do. She isn't going to believe this. Let me go wake her." Doona spoke quickly but kept her voice low.

"No, no," Peter said. "Let the poor woman sleep. We can see her in the morning."

Doona tilted her face forward, raising her eyebrows as if

Peter were a naughty child. Without a word, she swept out a different doorway.

"Robin is here?" Aizel asked.

"We can . . ." Peter's words were cut off by a fit of coughing.

Aizel stood, finding the hot water and cups that Doona had left on the table. She quickly brewed the tea leaves—which were darker than any she'd seen before—and handed the steaming cup back to Peter.

He took it from her, his coughs subsiding as he inhaled the warm steam. Lifting his free hand, he started to make a series of motions. "We can ask her to help Celesta."

Aizel understood his meaning perfectly before she even realized he had spoken to her with his hands. She sank back down to sit on the floor in front of the small fire. It felt so natural and so special to converse with someone this way. "Exactly what I was thinking," she responded. Peter was already thinking about how to free Celesta, although they hadn't even discussed it in the short span of hours they had known each other.

A few moments later, the door reopened, and a stocky young woman walked into the room. If she had truly just been sleeping, she didn't show it. She was wearing man's clothes that fit her particularly well. It made her look like a competent forest ranger, but a pretty one, with her light hair and stunning blue eyes.

She reached out and grabbed Peter's wrist, clasping his hand in an affectionate shake. "You look horrible." Her eyes were filled with concern.

"It's good to see you, too," Peter replied drily.

Aizel reached up and took the cup of tea from his hand as it threatened to spill over.

"I thought you were dead. This whole time. I'm so sorry, old friend." Robin let go of his hand and leaned her backside against the table behind her.

"I knew the risk," Peter responded. "Now stop looking at me like I'm that decrepit old donkey of yours and turn your attention to my wonderful companion. Robin—meet Aizel."

Robin reached down, holding out her hand like a man. Aizel reached out and grasped it firmly.

The woman said nothing. She merely observed Aizel closely before releasing her hand. Aizel didn't feel uncomfortable under her gaze. Rather, she felt as if she were reuniting with a long-lost friend. Everything about the other woman, from the way she dressed to the firm grip of her handshake, made Aizel feel more powerful. This woman was a hero, and she didn't care what other people thought of her.

"It looks like you two have a story to tell," Robin said.

Aizel nodded. "That's an understatement. But first . . ." As much as Aizel wanted to sit and rest—and get to know Robin —she was running out of time. She looked over to Peter.

He nodded encouragingly. "You have a voice."

Aizel smirked. She appreciated his words, but this was less about her voice and more about her pride. She turned back to Robin. "First, I need to ask for your help."

Robin said nothing, but her face and posture indicated she was listening.

"King Gareth has my younger sister, and he is going to take her life because I failed to take the life of Prince Erich of Iseldis." Aizel stopped to inhale. Nervousness flooded through her.

"A life for a life?" Robin crossed her arms and readjusted her weight against the table behind her. "That sounds like his twisted sense of justice. When is he planning to carry this out?"

"I don't know." Aizel's throat closed up. "It could have happened already. But we have to do something. I can use a bit of magic, but I don't know enough to storm the castle by myself—and I hate asking for help, but she is my best friend and she doesn't deserve this and I need to be there for her because it's mostly my fault." She stood up, realizing she sounded exactly as desperate as she was.

Robin's arms were still crossed. "The River's Talon has never stolen someone from under Gareth's nose directly, but I should think we are quite interested in giving it a try. It would be incredibly satisfying to accomplish." She smiled.

Aizel breathed again. "What can we do?"

"First, we need to find out where she is in the castle and what Gareth plans to do with her."

The back door crashed open as a young man dashed into the room. He closed the door behind him. "Gareth has scheduled an execution for tomorrow morning," he said, hunching over to catch his breath. He seemed completely unbothered by the group of people having a late-night discussion. "And, get this. It's for a Majis woman, or 'sorceress,' as he claims. What is he even thinking? I thought his whole goal was to inspire fear. But executing a Majis will make everyone feel less scared of them, won't it?"

"Well," Robin said, ignoring the man's monologue. "There's our answer." Her face had gone from compassionate to capable. "This doesn't leave us much time."

Aizel shook her head. "We don't have any time. Thanks for listening, but I'll just go straight back to Gareth and offer myself in Celesta's place. Keep Peter safe." Aizel slipped toward the door.

Robin grabbed her arm. "Wait. That is too risky and doesn't guarantee your sister's safety. You should at least consider a few other options."

"Such as?" Aizel felt tears building up behind her eyes.

"You have the ability to use magic," Robin said, "and I have a team of at least twelve, maybe fifteen people who are close enough to help. Let's see what we can do together."

CHAPTER 41

"The key, I have found," King Gareth said, "is to truly listen to your subjects. When they feel heard . . ."

Erich didn't care what the king was talking about. He was too busy planning his escape from the castle so he could find Aizel.

"Wouldn't you agree?" Gareth asked.

Erich nodded enthusiastically.

The door opened, and a young girl walked through.

For a moment, Erich stopped breathing. Had they already found her?

No. This girl was several years younger, and her hair and eyes were brown. She was wearing a white ribbon around her neck, which meant she was a Majis.

Erich relaxed. Aizel was still safe.

"This is the younger Majis," Gareth said. "She will take the blame for causing the latest sea storms, specifically the one that sank the ship you were on."

The young girl was watching Gareth closely, her forehead squinting lightly in concentration.

"I think the people will be more than happy to watch her die. It should restore some of their hope."

Erich snapped his head back to the king. "That's a little heartless to say right in front of her, don't you think?"

Gareth shrugged. "She can't hear, so she has no idea what I'm saying."

Erich looked back at the girl. He was certain he had seen a look of fear cross her face when Gareth mentioned her death.

His heart fell. He couldn't leave now, not when an innocent child was in danger.

"Can you hear me?" he mouthed at her, using his hand to point to her, his ear, and his mouth as Aizel would have done.

She shook her head, her eyes on his lips.

"What's going on?" she asked with her hands.

"I don't know," Erich responded. *"This man is a rotten person."* He made a face.

The girl laughed, covering her mouth while her shoulders shook.

Gareth said nothing. He merely watched the exchange.

"You can't truly mean to go through with this, Your Majesty," Erich said, turning back to him. "She's only a child. No one will believe she's a powerful sorceress."

Gareth shrugged once more. "She's a Majis."

The king's dismissive reaction reminded Erich of the time Gautho had used the same expression to dismiss something about Aizel.

This time, Erich knew better than to accept that excuse.

"I don't think this will inspire the trust you keep claiming," Erich argued, trying to appeal to the sentiments Gareth had mentioned. "What if they find out it was a lie?"

"And how would they discover that?"

"I . . . could tell them," Erich challenged. "Let her go," he pleaded. "She's innocent and harmless."

"The execution has already been scheduled. My hands are tied." Gareth sat back. "This girl's life is mine, and justice must be done."

"Justice?" Erich asked. "What kind of justice is this?"

"Do you disagree with me?" Gareth's tone was almost gleeful.

Erich closed his eyes. Aizel was free, and she had her voice. He wanted to make it out of this alive. He needed to bring this information to his father.

He looked at the little girl. Her eyes were staring at him, pleading with him.

He would never be able to forgive himself—or face Aizel—if he got out of this at the expense of this Majis child's life.

Aizel was strong and powerful and brave. She would find Robin and share what she knew. Erich wished he could have helped her. In a way, he was helping her. He was fighting for her and her people.

"If you want justice . . ." Erich turned to the king. "Would you take a life for a life?"

Gareth grinned. "What do you mean?"

"Let this girl go free and execute me in her place." Erich's voice was loud and clear, echoing off the smooth stone walls around him.

"Do you not agree with me?" Gareth asked again. He sounded disappointed, but his face was ecstatic.

"No!" Erich practically yelled. "You've been perpetuating lies throughout the entire kingdom for too long, and your goal of unity is really only a service to yourself. Someday, someone more powerful than I will expose you for the tyrant you are."

Gareth relaxed into his chair as if he had never been happier. "Thank you for your honesty, Erich of Iseldis. I accept your offer."

He waved a hand to the guards at the door. They stepped forward toward the girl.

"Wait," Erich said. "I am not so stupid as you might think."

"Hah!" Gareth stood. "You fit into my plan more perfectly than I dared hope. Chendas has been trying for decades to bring Iseldis to our way of thinking. Only as a united whole will the Five Kingdoms survive. But no, your father has always been too good for the Council, too good to be part of the whole. Now, my strategy is to weaken Iseldis until it is mine. How long do you think it will last when your family is dead?"

Erich stared back at the king, his breath unstable. "Let the girl go free." He made his voice as threatening as possible.

Gareth ignored him. "In a few hours, you will die in front of hundreds—thousands—of people. But with your face covered, they will have no idea who you actually are. Prince Erich of Iseldis, gone. Disappeared. It's perfect. Thank you for cooperating. Your sacrifice will indeed better the continent."

"Let the girl go free," Erich repeated.

"No need to sound so desperate," Gareth replied. "I always keep my word. Come."

Erich, flanked by four guards, followed Gareth and the girl to an empty courtyard at the back of the palace.

One of the guards removed the girl's necklace. She touched her neck, her eyes confused.

"Go," Gareth said, his voice unnaturally loud. "You're free."

She turned to Erich, her eyes filled with concern for him.

"Run," Erich mouthed. *"Run and don't stop running."*

She dipped her head. *"Thank you."* Then she turned and dashed through the gate.

Erich watched her until she was out of sight. He might have walked right into Gareth's plan, but he didn't regret his actions.

CHAPTER 42

"If you don't mind that they're used, I have an extra vest and cloak lying around here," Robin offered.

"Yes, please!" Aizel accepted with a smile. Seeing Robin's tactical clothing made Aizel far more confident in the black pants she was currently wearing. They had turned out to be quite warm and comfortable, and if someone as beautiful and brave as Robin could wear them with confidence, so could she.

Sinking into the tub of hot water Robin had requested, Aizel began to scrub the days of dirt and travel from her skin. Her hair was so matted in knots she was tempted to chop it all off rather than wash her way through it.

Eventually, as the water cooled around her, she felt a new type of confidence sink into her skin. The kind that came from feeling whole and fed and prepared.

She was ready to find Celesta and get her out of Gareth's clutches. And best of all, she didn't have to do it alone.

After drying herself, she added Robin's new layers to her current outfit, wishing she had a mirror to see herself in. She felt powerful, mobile, in control. And she loved it.

"Come in," Aizel called when a knock sounded at the door.

Robin entered, carrying a plain hat. "I think it would be smart to try to cover your hair. It's pretty unique and might draw unwanted attention."

"That sounds like a good idea to me."

Robin walked around her, looking from the hat to her hair. "Mhh. Would you mind if I braid it? I underestimated how much hair you have to hide."

"Not at all."

In a matter of moments, Robin had Aizel's hair braided and hidden under the hat. "I think we're ready."

Aizel took a deep breath. "Thank you," she said, hoping Robin understood she was talking about much more than the hat.

Robin nodded. "Let's go save Celesta."

As they made their way through the city streets, it was easy to blend in. People were all working their way in the same direction.

"Are Quotidian people always this excited to witness an execution?" Aizel's stomach churned.

"From what I hear, King Gareth prefers them to be well attended," Robin responded.

Aizel nodded. That answered her question, even if it didn't fully make sense. Occasionally, she caught a glimpse of other men and women dressed similarly to Robin weaving their way through the crowd. They were meant to be incon-spicuous, but Aizel knew what to look for.

None of them had slept the previous night as they had spent every moment perfecting their plan. It was risky, but if everyone played their part, it just might work.

Robin had left early in the morning to inform the other members of the River's Talon of their role.

Doona had fed them a hearty breakfast, and even Peter was participating, though his part would only come at the end.

Eventually, they arrived at a cobbled square in front of the marble palace. The white walls of the massive building were so bright, Aizel couldn't even look up at them. At the far end of the plaza, a wooden dais was set up. It was currently empty.

They'd arrived early, but the large area was already filling up.

Robin led Aizel around the edge of the square, pretending to look for a place for the two of them to settle.

"There," Aizel whispered, pointing discreetly toward a hooded figure standing near two shops. She couldn't see his face, but his hood was of the same fabric and design as the two Quotidian mages who had used their magic on her before they'd locked her up in the dungeon.

Robin strode forward, stopping near the man to yawn and stretch. After she walked away, two men who were also dressed in forester's clothing positioned themselves near the mage.

"This a good spot?" one of the men asked his companion.

"Perfect. Good view. Won't get trampled by the peasants," the other responded.

They continued to carry on a casual conversation as Aizel moved past them to follow Robin. Together, they made their way through the entire square, identifying at least five Quotidian mages and alerting members of the River's Talon to their presence.

"I'll meet you at the dais." Robin pulled a small chunk of wax from the sack on her belt.

Aizel nodded, swallowing her fear.

Robin was putting herself in the most dangerous position in case anything went wrong. Aizel was going to head back toward the square's opening to carry out her part of the magic.

With an encouraging smile on her face, Robin disappeared into the crowd.

Aizel wished they could have stayed together. The crowd was almost too dense to walk through, but she pushed herself back through it to get to her place.

The overwhelming noise of people's voices as they chatted in the square was enough to make Aizel wish she had thought to bring some wax of her own. She could sense the nervousness in the crowd as their voices climbed higher and higher in an attempt to be heard over one another.

This was going to be difficult.

By the time she got back to where they had started, a change of energy had come over the crowd.

Aizel peered back toward the dais, but she was too short to see anything through the crowds in front of her. She bounced on her tiptoes, catching a tiny glimpse of the dais.

Guards surrounded the edge, but a single figure knelt in the center of it. It looked as though they had put a cloth over Celesta's head.

Aizel's heart snapped. How dare they treat her sister this way? She wanted to stamp her foot into the ground and shout the angriest song she could think of. Or, better yet, she wished she could use Quotidian magic and bring these people to their knees in pain.

But she contented herself with balling her hands into fists.

Robin had told her to wait until after they started reading the proclamation. She'd said no one in the entire plaza would dare to make a noise while a messenger of the king was speaking. As soon as he finished, though, the plaza would erupt into cheers or jeering, and her song wouldn't be heard.

The crowd grew quiet, and Aizel could hear a distant voice coming from the direction of the dais.

Glancing to either side, she confirmed that Robin's companions were alert and ready near the two closest mages.

Aizel closed her eyes. Her whole body was shaking. This was a horrible idea. She'd never used magic on a scale this large before, and she didn't even know if it would work.

She squeezed her fists together, reminding herself of her favorite moments with Celesta—playing together, laughing together, making silent jokes behind their parents' backs . . . but every memory of her sister was tarnished by the intense fear she currently felt for Celesta's life.

The man's voice continued to drone on, and Aizel knew she was running out of time. She needed to find harmony within herself if this was going to work, though.

Unbidden, her mind brought up the image of Erich kneeling in the grass up in the mountains, promising to aid her. She had felt peace in that moment. But it wouldn't help now. She threw the thought away.

Her heart raced. She had to sing.

That memory of Erich would have to work. She put

herself back in that place, feeling her heart expand under the sincere gaze of his eyes.

She had found help, at least in Peter and Robin if not in Erich.

Calmed, she began to hum, so quietly she could barely hear it.

When she had attempted to sing in front of Gareth, she'd started as loudly as possible hoping that her power would increase with her volume. It hadn't worked as well as she'd thought, so she started quietly, as she had when she'd made the kitchen maids fall asleep.

She could feel the magic begin to work as her muscles relaxed, so she opened her mouth and began to sing instead of hum.

Her voice was confident, and her notes were pure.

She opened her eyes, singing a little louder.

Two of the townspeople in front of her turned back, looks of confusion on their faces. But their eyes quickly closed in drowsiness.

As the people around her slowly sank to the ground, she raised her voice again. They only had moments before the rest of the square would notice what was happening.

Projecting her song as far out as she could, Aizel slowly walked forward through the sleeping townspeople.

She noticed a scuffle out of the corner of her eye. One of the mages had caught on. She didn't dare turn and look, lest she get distracted. She had to trust that Robin's companions would be able to handle the situation.

People were falling asleep in greater numbers now, and she was nearly halfway across the square. By the time most of them realized what was going on, they were peacefully drowsing under her song.

The messenger had stopped reading the proclamation. He dropped the large parchment he was holding and dashed back toward the palace steps behind the dais.

The guards, too, had noticed what was happening, and a few of them jumped down and started heading her way.

Aizel inhaled, taking in as much air as her lungs would allow.

One of the guards reached forward, pressing Celesta's head down as though to speed up the actual execution.

Aizel sang louder than she ever had. Her clear voice hit the smooth, marble face of the palace and rippled back to her, carrying her voice farther than she could have ever done on her own.

Robin was on the dais now, sword drawn, sparring with the executioners.

The soldiers who were approaching her fell over in sleep.

It was working!

The entire square had collapsed in sleep!

Robin and her men had filled their ears with soft wax, so Aizel could still see them standing.

Quieting her voice, Aizel made her way through the sleeping bodies as fast as she could, rushing toward her sister.

But before she could reach the dais, one other figure stood out from the crowd. They were so short, Aizel hadn't noticed them.

Confused, Aizel stopped. She opened her mouth to sing once again when the small figure raised its arms in a wide arc over their head, wiggling their fingers all the way.

Celesta?

Aizel's heart pounded, and tears fell down her face.

Her sister was fine.

A new movement on the steps of the palace caught her attention, and Aizel noticed a fresh contingent of guards rushing down the steps. Behind them, a single figure stood, the crown on his brow sparkling in the sunlight.

Aizel ran toward her sister.

"Stop!" Celesta signed across the plaza. *"Save them"* She pointed to the dais where Robin was preparing to defend herself against the incoming soldiers.

"She's got this. She's a warrior." Aizel spoke with her hands as she continued racing toward Celesta.

"No, not her. Him." Celesta pointed back to the dais, where a sleeping figure with a covered face was sleeping among the soldiers.

But Aizel could only focus on one thing. *"No, you. Let's get out of here."*

"No!" Celesta's movements were as loud as she could make them. *"He saved me."* She moved away from Aizel, running toward the dais herself.

Aizel swerved back, struggling to find a safe place to put her feet among the sleeping bodies. She wanted to question her sister, to find out who had saved her. But she knew—somehow, deep inside her—whose face she would find under that cloth on the dais.

A clang of metal cut into her thoughts, and she looked up to see Robin fending off an entire group of soldiers on her own.

As impressive as it looked, Aizel knew it wouldn't last long.

Tapping into her relief that Celesta wasn't in immediate danger, Aizel opened her mouth and continued her song.

One by one, the soldiers around Robin fell to the ground.

Robin threw her a quick nod of thanks, then turned her attention back to the palace stairs, ready to face any new attackers.

Aizel reached the dais.

Celesta was slowly picking her way up the stairs, which were covered with collapsed people. Aizel used her upper arms—toned from years of swimming—to pull herself up over the side of the small stage, although she had to stop her song to do so.

Once on the higher platform, she could see the entire plaza more clearly. Her eyes noted the unusual sight of hundreds of people slumbering peacefully, though her mind had no time to marvel at it.

Another group of soldiers poured down the palace steps. Behind them stood King Gareth, his hands covering his ears. She could barely make out the look of rage on his face, but she could feel the smug satisfaction that rose inside of her.

She quickly wound her way to the stranger's side, singing as she went to help Robin with the remaining soldiers.

Grabbing the rough-woven cloth from the stranger's face with one hand, she lifted his heavy head with the other and tugged the cloth free.

The sight of Erich's face, calm and peaceful, overwhelmed her so much she stopped singing.

He had saved her sister. He had taken Celesta's place. She had no idea how he'd done it, nor how she would ever repay him.

"Aizel!" Robin called. "We need to get out of here. NOW."

Aizel looked up. A line of archers stood beside the king on the top step. They wore coverings over their ears.

Looping her hands under Erich's arms, Aizel tugged him

toward the edge of the dais. Celesta was at her side, pushing his sleeping body toward the edge.

Jumping down, Aizel pulled Erich on top of her.

He landed awkwardly across her bent back.

She grabbed whatever part of him she could and slowly made her way to a side entrance of the square.

An arrow whizzed past her head.

She flinched but kept moving.

Another flew by. She wasn't going to make it out of this. Wait—that arrow had been going the wrong direction. It had been traveling toward the king's archers.

Aizel looked up. Members of the River's Talon were hiding on roofs and in the upper levels of the buildings surrounding her, covering her exit.

Robin appeared at her side, looping one of Erich's arms over her shoulder.

Together, they traveled twice as fast. Celesta followed beside them.

"Aizel, sing!" Robin called.

Clinging to Erich, Aizel opened her mouth, jumping straight to her favorite verse of the song. She didn't need to turn around to know that more soldiers were following them.

The side entrance was far nearer than the one Aizel had come from, and they reached it quickly.

Just outside the entrance, a wooden carriage sat waiting. Peter hopped down from the driver's seat and helped them lift Erich into the carriage. Aizel and Celesta climbed up after him.

"Go," Robin said. "I'll see my men and women to safety, then find you at the rendezvous point."

The sound of the carriage wheels rolling across the dirt road drowned out her last words.

"Thank you!" Aizel called.

Pulling Erich further into the carriage, she turned to her sister.

Celesta threw her arms around Aizel, and they both burst into tears.

CHAPTER 43

$\mathcal{E}$rich was sure he was dead.

Fortunately, he didn't remember any pain during the dying part, so that was nice.

He currently felt no pain, either—which was why he was convinced he must be dead.

He exhaled and opened his eyes, curious to see what the afterlife looked like.

Interesting. He hadn't expected it to look like the evergreen trees in the mountains above Chendas. He didn't mind. The trees were beautiful.

Not quite as beautiful as Aizel, though. He missed Aizel. Maybe he would see her here again someday. Were there days in the afterlife? He would have to find someone and ask. But, for the moment, he would just enjoy lying on his back and looking up at the beautiful trees.

Then, someone leaned over him. Someone who looked remarkably similar to Aizel.

His eyes widened. It was Aizel.

"Did you die, too?" He felt both sad for her and happy for himself at the same time.

"You have some explaining to do," she said. Her beautiful green eyes were glaring at him. "Last time we spoke, you were heading back to Iseldis and your family. Then suddenly you were striding into King Gareth's palace in that horrible gray uniform."

Erich scrunched his face, trying to recall the events she was referencing. "You're alive!" He looked back at her as the last horrible hours of his life came crashing back into his memory. She was alive, and if the forest canopy above him was any indicator, they were both safe.

"Explain yourself." If she was as angry as she looked, he would not be safe for much longer.

"I am so sorry, Aizel. I immediately started back toward the mountains, but General Gautho accosted me a few hours after we separated. Knowing now that he was on Gareth's side in all this, he was probably tracking us to make sure everything went according to their plan. He dragged me back as a prisoner. I promise."

"I thought you'd betrayed me." Her voice was barely more than a whisper.

"I will never betray you," he promised. He wanted to pull her into a hug, to reassure her that he would always be there for her. But this was not the right moment.

Her eyes searched his.

"I promise," he said.

Her face relaxed. "I want to believe you."

"Is it really that horrible?" he asked.

"What?"

"The gray uniform?" He wanted to make her smile.

"Yes!" Her face lit up. "It's awful. It makes you all stiff and overbearing."

"I've always hated that thing, and I'm so glad someone finally agrees with me." He smiled up at her beautiful face. "You're positive I'm not dead?"

"No, silly, you're not dead." Her beautiful red hair was all braided up. It fell over her shoulder and dangled in front of his face. "Although you should be. And I'm so happy you're not that I could kiss you."

"Do," Erich responded instantly. Although if she was volunteering to kiss him, maybe he was dreaming.

Aizel leaned over him, her braid brushing his cheek as she drew nearer. Then, her lips pressed against his. They were softer than he'd ever imagined, and his whole body jumped to life.

He was most definitely alive and awake.

She lifted her head, a small smile dancing in her green eyes.

Reaching his hands up, Erich slipped them behind her neck and gently nudged her face back toward his.

She laughed and kissed him again.

A content sigh escaped Erich's mouth when she finally pulled away. As he pushed himself up from the ground, the whole world shifted into place below him. "I'm dead," he announced. "I'm dead. I'm dead. I'm dead."

"You saved my sister's life," Aizel said. "So, I returned the favor by saving yours. Again."

"Your sister?" Erich asked, looking around for the little Majis girl with brown hair. "That was your sister?"

"Celesta," Aizel said, moving her hands in an arc over her head as she spoke.

"Where is she?" Erich asked, suddenly alarmed. They

were in a small pocket of the mountainous forest, and it was quite empty. "Is she alright? Did she find safety?"

"Yes." Aizel reached her hands out toward him. "Thanks to you. And me. And Robin."

"You found Robin of Lockwood?" Erich looked around the empty clearing once more.

Aizel nodded. "She'll be here shortly. Hopefully. Peter and Celesta went to watch for her." Aizel glanced to her right, worry creeping into her face.

Erich grabbed her extended hands with one of his and reached up to tentatively stroke her cheek with the other. His heart fell as he recalled the last time he had seen her. He'd thrown himself at the hooded men who were hurting her with Quotidian magic, but the king's guards had removed him from the room. "Are you alright?"

The smile she gave him was more brilliant than her sparkling hair. "Yes. I used my magic to make hundreds of people fall asleep all at once. I love using my voice, and I'm never going to let anyone silence me again. Celesta is safe, for now, and I'll never leave her side again."

"I never want to leave your side again," Erich whispered, losing his sanity in the depths of her big green eyes. "I would wed you in a heartbeat and never regret it."

Her eyes opened even wider.

"I mean, no. Forget I said anything. I would never presume to be worthy of you." He dropped his hand from her face and glanced toward the ground. "You probably hate me. And for good reason, since I've been an absolute terror to you and I'm rather a dunce and I clearly don't deserve you and I would never ask you to love me after everything I've put you through."

"I don't."

Erich's shoulders dropped. "Yeah, that makes sense. Well, at least come back to Iseldis with me and we'll get you and your sister to safety. Or, wherever you want to go."

"I don't hate you."

Erich lifted his eyes to her face.

"I did hate you. And you were awful." She squeezed his hand, closing the small distance between them. "But that was before I knew you."

Erich froze, afraid to move a single muscle in his body. "You don't hate me?"

"Do you need me to repeat it again?" She smiled up at him. "You are rather a dunce."

"I'm so sorry, Aizel," Erich said. He wanted to drop his eyes from her face, to hide his stupidity and shame from the woman in front of him. But he kept his eyes on hers. She had to know how truly he had grown and changed from their journey together.

"Erich." Her face still held a smile, but it was tender instead of teasing. "I don't want another apology."

"What do you want?" Erich asked. "What can I do for you to ever make it up to you?"

Aizel shook her head. "You've still got it all wrong. You've given me so much."

Erich inhaled, wishing her words to be true.

"You've given me hope. That things could change for me. For Celesta."

Erich etched her words into his memory so that he would never forget them. "I will do everything in my power to give your sister the best life she could ever dream of. And anything else you could ever ask of me, I will give to you. Wherever you wish to go, what ever you wish to do, you have only to ask and I will move all of Iseldis to serve you. To know that you do not hate me is enough."

"I don't hate, you." She leaned forward, bringing her face directly below his. "And I would never ask you to serve me. But I would be honored to give you my love. To never again leave your side."

"But why?" He could not believe the words he was hearing. "I've been awful to you!"

"Even in the very beginning, your words might have been cruel, but your actions were not. When something wasn't right, you never rested until you'd learned more about it. I like that. I've never seen that in someone before, and you manage to combine it with being the most fun and colorful person I've ever met. I love you now. I don't care if you change—please keep changing—as long as you don't stop trying to learn. That's all I ask."

"You're serious?" Erich took in her whole face.

She was completely serious.

"You deserve so much better than me," Erich whispered, afraid to lose what she was offering him.

"Do you love me?"

"So much," Erich replied. "You are so brave and good and selfless. You showed me the world in a whole new way, and I will be forever thankful for that. You taught me things about myself that I didn't even know, and I am forever changed because of it. I owe you so much. You deserve so much, and I want to give you a better world. One that sees you the way I do."

"I don't need you to give it to me," she replied. "But I would love to build that world with you, side by side."

"Together?"

"Forever," she whispered.

Dropping his head, Erich pressed his lips against hers. He poured himself into the kiss, silently pledging his life to keep her safe and happy.

She threw her arms around his neck, twisting her body to fall perfectly into his lap.

"Oh!" Robin's voice called out from close by. "Pardon us for interrupting."

With a final taste of her lips, Erich turned his head to greet the small party entering the clearing.

"Robin!" Aizel jumped up. "You're safe." She threw herself into the other woman's arms.

It wasn't until then that Erich realized Aizel was wearing a woodsman's trousers. He smiled. They suited her. Or rather, she suited them. She was perfect in anything.

"Robin, this is Erich," Aizel introduced them. "He's a prince and my future husband." As she spoke, she moved her hands to include her younger sister in the conversation.

Celesta clapped her hands at the announcement.

"Congratulations!" Robin stepped forward past Aizel and held out her hand to Erich.

Erich shook her hand, smiling awkwardly. "Hello, Robin."

"It seems we have some catching up to do, little brother," she whispered with a wink. Then, louder so everyone could hear, "When is this grand wedding to take place?"

"If we had a monk or minister, here and now!" Erich said, making a jest but wishing it were true.

A deep voice sounded from the small crowd of people still pouring into the glade.

Erich looked over Robin's shoulder to see a rotund man in monk's robes step forward.

Robin smiled. "Brother Fletcher, I think he might have been jesting."

Erich raised his eyebrows at Aizel.

She lifted her shoulders in a cute little shrug and danced back to his side, grabbing his hand. "I've already hauled your sleeping body to safety twice. We might as well make it official before you get yourself in trouble again."

"Are you certain?" Erich whispered.

"Are you?"

"I've never been so certain of anything in my life."

CHAPTER 44

*E*rich led his tired crew through the family gate of the Iseldis courtyard.

Robin and her companions had left them a week prior, disappearing to carry out their own business. Peter had opted to come all the way to Iseldis with them, saying he had family in the area.

"Remember," Aizel whispered up to Erich as they slipped from their horses. "Robin asked us not to mention her by name."

He nodded and hoped he actually remembered not to slip up this time.

Celesta held Peter's hand. She was practically falling asleep on her feet.

"Well," Erich said, "let's go meet the family." He was nervous for the conversations to come, but he was thrilled to have Aizel at his side.

The door to the castle opened and Meena flew out,

running across the courtyard. She threw herself at Erich in a hug that involved several playful punches. "How dare you leave me without saying goodbye? How dare you!" she yelled. "Never, ever do that again."

Erich hugged her back. "Meena, I would like you to meet . . ." He paused for dramatic effect. "My wife."

The shriek in his ear nearly deafened him.

Meena jumped from his arms and immediately threw herself at Aizel.

"While I introduce her to the family," Erich asked, "could you take her younger sister Celesta and find some food, maybe a hot bath and some warm clothes?" Erich used his hands along with his voice so Celesta could understand what was happening. He had gotten much better at speaking with his movements over their long trip back through the mountains.

Celesta smiled shyly at his exuberant sister.

Meena leaned down to bring herself eye level with the young girl. "Would you like something delicious to eat?" She copied Erich's motion, indicating her mouth.

Celesta nodded, happily slipping her hand into Meena's.

Erich led Aizel and Peter to his parents' private salon, where his father and mother joined them in a heartbeat. After more hugs, Erich grabbed Aizel's hand and pulled her forward.

"Father. Mum. This is Aizel, my wife. She's from the Isle of Istroya. And she's a Majis."

Erich watched his parents' carefully schooled faces.

"You didn't have to lead with that," Aizel whispered with a hiss.

"Best to rip the linen off the wound, as the healers would say." Erich smirked back.

Queen Cara stepped forward, pulling Aizel into a gentle hug, but Erich didn't miss the glare she sent his father over Aizel's shoulder.

"It would seem we have much to catch up on," King Frederich said, raising his eyebrows at Erich.

"You have no idea." Erich smiled at his father. Perhaps it would be more fun than anticipated to share everything he had learned.

The door opened behind them and Ian entered, followed closely by Onric and his sweetheart, Ashlin.

Erich braced himself for more hugs as Ian and Onric threw themselves at him.

Behind them, Ashlin had gone completely pale. Her eyes were glued to Peter's face.

"Papa?" she whispered. Then, in two leaps, she flung herself into the older man's arms as a strangled cry left her lips.

Peter somehow managed to keep his balance as his daughter squeezed his body with everything she had.

"You're alive. You're alive," she repeated, tears streaming down her face.

Erich blinked, realizing his cheeks were getting a little wet, too. Aizel reached for his hand.

His brother Onric stepped forward as Ashlin finally took half a step away from her father. Erich had a feeling she wouldn't allow anyone to move the man away for some time.

"My sweet, sweet girl," Peter said, pulling her back in for another hug. "I never thought I'd see you again."

Noticing Onric close by, Ashlin reached her hand out toward him. "Father, this is Onric."

Peter kept his arm firmly around his daughter's shoulders. "Yes, I know who His Highness is. But I would like to know why you're here at the palace with him." He raised his eyebrows.

"That's a bit of story." Ashlin's face clouded over as she looked down. "And not all of it is good."

Peter placed a hand on her cheek. "Your stepmother?"

Ashlin nodded, still avoiding his eyes.

He pressed her face against his chest. "I am so sorry. So, so sorry. I started helping the Majis soon after your mother died." He glanced up at Erich's father, as if remembering too late he shouldn't be mentioning outlawed activities in front of a king. "I was going to share the mission with Meliora, but every time I planned to tell her, something felt off. I never fully trusted her. The enormity of that didn't fully hit me until I realized you were alone with her." He leaned back, taking Ashlin's face in both hands and peering into her eyes. "I hope she hasn't been too terrible?"

Onric stepped forward, reaching out and touching the back of Ashlin's hand as if to let her know he was there.

She instantly wrapped her hand around his, holding on to him for support.

Erich smiled at the tiny interaction. He doubted that anyone else in the room had even noticed it, but it was typical of his older brother. Onric was the most solid of any of them, and Ashlin had completely stolen his heart.

He squeezed Aizel's hand. Ashlin was great and all, but she wasn't nearly as fun as his fiercely independent and daring Aizel.

"It's a bit of a tale, sir," Onric answered Peter's earlier question. "Perhaps one best saved for a more private moment."

Ashlin smiled at Onric with appreciation.

"Of course," Peter said.

"Why don't we all get comfortable?" King Frederich gestured to the circle of chairs and sofas in the room. "I believe you all have some explaining to do."

CHAPTER 45

*L*ater that night, after a long, fruitful discussion with the king and queen, Aizel followed Erich through the dim hallways of the castle to a bedroom on the upper floor.

A small fire was already lit in the open stone fireplace, and the most comfortable bed she had ever seen sat against the far wall.

If she had seen that many pillows on a single bed at any other time in her life, she would have scoffed. But after spending weeks sleeping on the hard ground, she would take every possible pillow she could get.

"Are you tired?" he asked.

She turned to him, holding his hand between both of hers. "I'm tired, but I'm not very sleepy." His father had been very receptive to their information. Although he had struggled to believe the truth of it, he had promised to speak with them more in the following days.

Erich's eyebrows pinched together. "I have a slight problem, wife, that I haven't told you about yet."

"What is it?" Aizel kept her voice kind because she wasn't in the least bit concerned. After everything they had been through together, she was sure they could handle any obstacle.

"I have one tiny regret about marrying you." Erich held up his fingers to indicate just how tiny the regret was.

"Oh really?" She crossed her arms. He had better be jesting.

"I've only ever had one skill that I required in my future wife, and I rather forgot to ask you about it earlier."

"And what would that be?" She scratched the back of her neck as she flipped her hair over her shoulder. Twisting it down in front of her, she took a step toward Erich to close the distance between them.

He grinned down at her, pausing as long as he possibly could before answering her question. "Dancing."

"Dancing?" That wasn't at all what she had expected. But coming from Erich, it somehow made perfect sense.

"I've always wanted to spend my life with someone who loved dancing. So . . . Aizel of Istroya and Princess of Iseldis, do you like to dance?"

Aizel had not spent much of her life dancing, but that was a problem she was happy to solve. "I love dancing. Although it might be one area in which you can teach me something."

"Oh, good." Erich sighed dramatically, dropping his shoulders as he swiped his forehead. "You had me stressed there for a second. Here I was worrying that we'd made a rash decision we would both regret."

"Do you regret it?" Standing up on her tiptoes, Aizel placed her hands against his chest to steady herself as she brought her face as close to his as possible.

"Not even for a second. You are perfect for me, and I'll do my best to be the same for you." He leaned down to bring their faces together.

"I don't need you to be perfect. I just need you to be by my side, standing next to me and fighting with me. Forever."

"Done." He tilted his face to the side, rubbing her nose with his as he brought their lips together.

She slipped her hand behind his neck, enjoying his closeness as she responded to his kiss.

He put his hand on her waist and lifted his head. "Dance with me?"

"Right now?"

He nodded.

"We don't have any music."

"We don't need music."

Aizel held up her finger, motioning for him to be quiet.

She placed one hand on his shoulder and the other in his open hand. Stepping into his embrace, she placed her head against his chest.

She could hear his heartbeat, and she felt her own heart pulsing in time with his. This was right. Everything outside was strangled in chaos, and they still had so much work to do, but inside the four walls of this castle bedroom, everything was right.

Closing her eyes, she began to hum, making up the notes as she went. It was a quiet song, but it was fueled by the combined beating of their hearts.

Erich placed a kiss on the top of her head, then began to sway in time with her tune. As he found his footing, he pulled her into the dance, swinging her around but always drawing her back into the comforting circle of his arms.

EPILOGUE

"Meena." Her brother's voice sounded outside Meena's door.

She cracked open the door.

"I have to talk to you," Erich said, his voice quiet and conspiratorial.

"Why are you whispering? Everyone else has been awake for hours." She wanted to run up and down the hall, screaming in happiness that Erich had finally returned. She'd nearly died from crying when he'd been shipwrecked all those weeks ago.

"Everyone else hasn't been sleeping on sticks and stones for nights on end. Aizel and I can sleep all day if we want to, but that's not the point. Quit distracting me. I'm whispering because I have to talk to you about something."

Meena felt tears building up in her eyes all over again. She'd missed him so much. "Alright, I guess you can come in for a second." She rolled her eyes as she opened the door for him to enter.

"Aizel needs clothes," Erich said as soon as the door was closed behind him.

"That's not a problem," Meena responded. "We can send for Mistress Cedrice and Ashlin."

"I already did," Erich replied. "But it will take days to fit her and sew new things. I want her to have something now. Don't you have a few dresses you can spare?"

Meena felt her whole face light up. "You want me to dress her?"

"Yes! Would you?"

"I would love to." Meena did not have to force her enthusiasm.

"I thought you might." Erich instantly relaxed. "She likes flowers, especially clovers."

"Clovers?"

"Yes. You know, those light purple spherical ones that grow in the forest?" Erich explained.

"I know what clovers are," Meena responded, tempted to roll her eyes again.

"What's wrong with clovers?" Erich looked offended.

"Nothing, I was just surprised," Meena replied. "I don't think I have anything with clovers on it specifically, but I do have a few purple dresses. Those would go quite well with her red hair—"

"Exactly what I was thinking," Erich said, cutting her off.

Meena clapped her hands. "This will be fun. Go get her now!"

A few moments later, Aizel was sitting on the edge of Meena's bed, her eyes wide in awe as she stared at the light purple dress Meena held up.

"Do you like it?" Meena asked.

"It's beautiful," Aizel said. "But I can't take one of your dresses."

"It's not mine anymore," Meena responded. "It's yours. I grew out of it a few years ago, but you're a bit shorter than me." She held the dress up to prove her point. The hem was a good length from the ground. "Come on, let's try it on and see if it fits."

"Are you sure?" Aizel's words were hesitant, but Meena could see a sparkle in her eyes.

"Absolutely sure!"

Aizel stood from the bed and started to take off her boyish clothing.

"Erich told me you saw Robin?" Meena asked, eager for news of her old friend.

"He said you were the only one he could share that with," Aizel responded.

"Does she need help?" Meena asked. She had heard Erich and Aizel's story the previous night, and she had needed far less convincing than her father.

"Of course she does. She's doing far too much by herself," Aizel responded, slipping the purple dress over her head.

"I want to help her," Meena said, helping to tie the laces in the back of the dress. "I want to help you."

Aizel twisted around, catching Meena's gaze. "If you're serious, I will talk to Erich about letting you in on our plans."

"I'm deadly serious," Meena responded. Her heart thumped erratically. She was scared, but she could not sit by while innocent people were being harmed. Little Celesta had instantly captured her heart the night before, and she was absolutely sick to think of the danger the innocent girl had been in.

Meena twirled Aizel back around to finish tying the laces.

The purple dress fit the smaller woman perfectly. Aizel spun in a circle, a smile on her face as her fingers ran over the floral embroidery on the sleeves and neckline.

"How about a necklace?" Meena grabbed a gold chain from a shelf in her room.

Aizel waved her away. "No, I don't particularly like necklaces."

Meena dropped the chain. "You look amazing." She'd always wanted a sister, and she couldn't wait to spend more time with Aizel.

"Thank you for the dress," Aizel said.

Meena smiled. "Erich!" she called, raising her voice.

Just as she'd expected, Erich stepped immediately into the room as though he'd been waiting right outside the door.

"I've never seen anything so beautiful," Aizel said, spinning around again.

"Neither have I," Erich said.

Meena smiled. She had a feeling he was talking about a lot more than the dress.

ACKNOWLEDGMENTS

To my real life friend, Aizel, thank you for letting me borrow your beautiful name for Ariel in this story. The character and her flaws are entirely my own, but I like to think she gets her singing voice from you.

Thanks Amelia for reading everything I send you! You are so fast and always positive. Seriously couldn't do this without you!

Thank you Judith for your many hours of proofreading, and Mariëlle for your grammar expertise!

And Ethan, there's a little piece of you in every hero that I write. Thanks for giving me plenty of inspiration. ;)

READY FOR MEENA'S STORY?

A fake marriage.

At least, for one of them.

Meena is in love. It happened quite suddenly, and with the most unexpected person. He's quiet and serious and completely unlike her constantly teasing brothers. The only problem? He has no idea she exists.

Sol is a Majis. He's spent his whole life in survival mode. He doesn't take risks and he doesn't like to be seen. But the world is changing, and he can't hide any longer.

Now that King Gareth knows his secret is out, Meena concocts the perfect plan. As a husband and wife—even if it's fake—she and Sol can stealthily unravel their enemy's latest plan.

ABOUT THE AUTHOR

Emily Deady grew up as an avid reader who hated writing. One day she realized that most authors loved cats and tea, her two favorite things. So, she stopped fighting the inevitable and she began to write. Her stories contain a generous helping of romance with a sprinkle of magic.

She loves growing things in dirt, brewing lightly roasted oolongs, chatting with her real-life hero who patiently listens to all her plotlines, and hitting the trails for a hike in sunny San Diego.

If you would like to connect with her directly, click here join her email newsletter where she has a tendency to give away free stories.